Gene Wolfe's

The Book of the New Sun

A Chapter Guide

Michael Andre-Driussi

DEDICATION

To Gene Wolfe (1931-2019)

I started this project in late 2018 as a "long goodbye" to Gene Wolfe. His passing away on Palm Sunday of 2019 was very sudden to me, much sooner than I expected.

I learned a great deal from him. Reading *The Book of the New Sun* led me to read a lot of other books, from Dickens to Proust to the Bible. In many ways Gene Wolfe taught me the way to read.

Gene Wolfe was generous with his time. I corresponded with him by mail for many years. I met him personally seven times. I miss him, but sometimes I have to remind myself he is gone.

CONTENTS

ACKNOWLEDGMENTS

In my GEnie days (1991-1996?) I discussed the fiction of Gene Wolfe with Greg Feeley, Neil Gaiman, Joe Mayhew, Michael Swanwick, and Jeff Wilson, among others.

I published *Lexicon Urthus* in 1994. The Lexicon brought me letters from David Langford.

It also brought me friendship with Alice K. Turner (1939-2015), and she talked me into joining the Urth List in 1997. There I met many, but for this application I will limit the roll to Marc Aramini, Robert Borski, Craig Brewer, Bill Carmichael, Roy C. Lackey, Jonathan Laidlow, Dan Parmenter, Nigel Price, Pedro Jorge Romero, and James Wynn.

INTRODUCTION

This work is a chapter-by-chapter reading guide to *The Book of the New Sun*, its sequel *The Urth of the New Sun,* and four stand-alone Urth stories ("The God and His Man," *Empires of Foliage and Flower,* "The Cat," and "The Map").

The Guide is a literary supplement for *Lexicon Urthus,* but it does not replace *Lexicon Urthus,* nor does it reuse much of the Lexicon.

The Guide is intended to be used by first time readers of *The Book of the New Sun* as well as those who are reading it again. The idea is that we are reading it together, you and I. There are no spoilers, but things will be noted as they are revealed.

How To Use The Guide
A reader could read a chapter of the source text first, then check in this book for the notes.

Or

A reader could read this book directly.

Pattern Recognition
For this project I follow the lead established by John Clute, Greg Feeley, and Neil Gaiman. Clute, through several Wolfe-related pieces gathered in his collection *Strokes* (1988), taught me an atomic level of inspection and blazed the trail to the Apollo thread of Severian's narrative. Feeley, in a single two-part essay ("The Evidence of Things Not Shown: Family Romance in *The Book of the New Sun,*" *The New York Review of Science Fiction No. 31* and *No. 32,* 1991), exposed the literature level of sentence and scene, which might be termed the molecular mode, by citing text traces to such wildly different authors as Shakespeare, James Blish, and Harlan Ellison. Gaiman, through discussion on the GEnie BBS beginning in 1992, shared the excellent strategy of "find the author" in genial-general and stunning-specific.

1

These three were in correspondence with each other, sharing notes and ideas, such that at times it becomes difficult to determine the origin point for a particular notion.

VOLUME I: THE SHADOW OF THE TORTURER

A thousand ages in thy sight
  Are like an evening gone;
Short as the watch that ends the night
  Before the rising sun.

Epigraph: From Wolfe's article "Hands and Feet" (*Castle of Days*, 228), the epigraph comes from "Psalm XC" by poet Isaac Watts (1674-1748). This poem, based upon Psalm 90, was collected in *The Psalms of David* (1719). The relevant verse in the King James Version goes like this: "For a thousand years in thy sight are but as yesterday when it is past, and as a watch in the night" (Psalm 90:4).

1. Resurrection and Death

Severian, an apprentice torturer, after nearly drowning in the River Gyoll, has difficulty gaining access to the locked graveyard that he and his friends must pass through to return home, until apprentice Drotte plays a psychological trick on the volunteers. Once inside the graveyard, Severian has a chance encounter with the exultant rebel Vodalus and his henchmen robbing a grave. He spontaneously aids the outlaw by killing a volunteer guard. Severian ends the chapter by declaring that his narrative will describe how he "backed into the throne."

Chapter Title: The phrase has a reversal, where the wording is usually "death and resurrection." Here the "resurrection" is a bodysnatching ("resurrectionist" is a euphemistic term for graverobbers in 18th and 19th century British English), and the "death" is that of two volunteers trying to prevent grave robbing.

Myth: Gyoll (10) in the Norse system is the river of death.

3

Melville: Relevant to the entry above about an allusion to myth, Ursula K. Le Guin famously called Gene Wolfe "our Melville." Presumably she was referring to Herman Melville's technique of using allusions. The opening of *Moby Dick* (1851) is the famous line, "Call me Ishmael," a Biblical allusion that gives backstory with the swiftness of a lightning strike. Within that same paragraph the narrator mentions the suicide of Cato the Younger, linking to *Plutarch's Lives* (second century AD). The chapter goes on with bits about the Roman Stoics, Greek myth, Milton's *Paradise Lost*, and even the philosophical religion of the Pythagoreans. Wolfe uses a similar approach in *The Book of the New Sun*, as we will see in the course of this Guide.

Mark Twain: Drotte's con job with the volunteers is worthy of Tom Sawyer. After Eata darts through the gate, Drotte claims they are herb gatherers, but then when the volunteers are still resistant, he says, "If you won't let us gather the herbs, we'd better go. I don't think we could ever find that boy in there now" (11).

But there is more Twain to this chapter than just that. The novel *The Adventures of Tom Sawyer* (1876) has a pivotal scene in a graveyard. It is in chapter 9, when Tom and Huck go out to the cemetery at night to perform experiments with a dead cat. There they chance upon a trio who have just robbed a grave of its corpse. An argument among the thieves, which leads to murder, is witnessed in secret by the boys. This incident propels the rest of the novel.

Dickens: Severian meeting Vodalus in the necropolis (13) echoes the first chapter of Charles Dickens's *Great Expectations* (1861) where young Pip encounters the convict Magwitch in a graveyard. In his 1991 essay, Greg Feeley denotes this Dickensian allusion "oft-remarked" (*New York Review of Science Fiction No. 32,* p. 13).

Paradoxes to Perfect Memory: "Roche or Drotte?" In the first pages, when the apprentices are outside the necropolis, Severian writes: "Roche held me, saying, 'Wait, I see pikes'" (10). A few paragraphs later, Severian makes his first allusion to his unusual memory: "(which in the final accounting loses nothing)," yet in the next paragraph Severian writes, "but they had pikes, as Drotte had said."

So which is it: Roche, or Drotte?

This curious situation was first noted on the Urth List by Bill Carmichael (18 OCT 1999). It spurred Roy C. Lackey into tracking, and he came up with a theory: "Whenever in the text Severian starts vaunting his perfect memory, not always, but often enough, that the particular memory then recounted, or another close by in the text, will be flawed" (9 JUL 2003).

In this manner, the perfect memory of Severian is paradoxed.

Animal Form: Thea's voice is likened to a dove's call (13); Thea herself is described as a dove, while the heavy man is announced an arctother, a cave bear.

Commentary: The three volunteers facing Vodalus are the leader, armed with a long knife (10), to whom Drotte had spoken (10-11; 15); the pikeman (15) who runs away (16); and the man with the ax, whom Severian kills. The axman might be the one who had said "I'm going to watch over my mother" (12), and thus he was probably the son of the dead woman whose body was taken away.

Robert Graves: The detail of an unlikely character "backing into the throne" probably sparks C. N. Manlove in 1986 to detect an *I, Claudius* (1934) angle to Severian's narrative (*Science Fiction: Ten Explorations,* p. 201).

2. Severian

Severian claims to have perfect memory. He tells of living on Citadel Hill in the city of Nessus. He describes the orphan status of all the apprentices, and how he has made a mausoleum into his own private fort. The symbols above his mausoleum's ancient door are a fountain, a flying ship, and a rose.

Earlier in that same day he met Vodalus, he had nearly drowned while swimming in the River Gyoll, but after a near-death dream-vision involving the ghost of Master Malrubius, he was saved by an undine.

Borges: Jorge Luis Borges's short story "Funes the Memorius" (1942), involving a young man with prodigious memory, is in 1983 cited by John Clute, collected in *Strokes* (152) as relating to Severian's memory.

Wolfe mentions the influence of Borges's book *The Book of Imaginary Beings* in his article "Onomastics, the Study of Names" (*Castle of Days,* 253). During an interview with Joan Gordon, Wolfe mentions three Borges stories: "Rosendo's Tale," "Doctor Brodie's Report," and "Tlön, Uqbar, Orbis Tertius" (Wright's *Shadows of the New Sun,* 28). He mentions "The Library of Babel" in his article "Books in *The Book of the New Sun*" (ibid, 193).

Clark Ashton Smith: Smith's "Xothique" stories of the 1930s are seen as precursors to Jack Vance's *The Dying Earth* (1950). While Vance does not have much truck with torturers, Smith has "The Isle of the Torturers" (1933), but these people are technically sadists who prey upon random travelers rather than being the punishment section of the justice arm of a government. Smith's torturers are not the heroes of his story, either.

> Uccastrog, which lay far to the east of Cyntrom, was commonly known as the Isle of the Torturers; and men said that all who landed upon it unaware, or were cast thither by the seas, were imprisoned by the inhabitants and were subjected later to unending curious tortures whose infliction formed the chief delight of these cruel beings. (*Zothique,* p. 224)

During an interview with Larry McCaffery, Wolfe mentions Clark Ashton Smith in a list of genre authors he admires (Wright's *Shadows of the New Sun,*

98) and acknowledges his debt to Smith during an interview with James B. Jordan (ibid, 104).

Myth: "Nessus" (20) comes from Greek myth, where it is the name of the centaur who murdered Heracles with a poisoned shirt.

Poe: That Severian has a mausoleum he calls his own (21) seems like a detail from the morbid Romanticism of Edgar Allan Poe, most closely the poem "Annabel Lee" (1849), where the living narrator sleeps every night in the tomb of his beloved.

Contrast: The first chapter gave an impression of adventure among boarding school boys, something along the lines of Rudyard Kipling's *Stalky & Co.* (1899), but now it becomes clear that the boys are in training to be torturers. This is a bracing contrast, as nostalgia for childhood gives way to somber gothic pondering.

Commentary: Regarding the details of Severian's near-drowning in the River Gyoll, note the roots, "as fine and strong as hair" (24), and how they left Severian feeling "caught in a hundred nets" (25); consider the curious disorientation, such that he "no longer knew in what direction the surface lay" (25); then comes the vision of Malrubius; and finally the undine grasped him, "then flung me down . . . down into the blackness until at last I struck what I took to be the bottom mud and burst through it into a world of light" (26).

3. The Autarch's Face

It becomes evident that Severian's tower is a grounded rocket ship.

Severian examines the coin Vodalus gave him, finding on one side what he first takes to be a woman's face, while the other side has a flying ship exactly like the one at his mausoleum door. He hides the coin and reflects on his guild.

Dickens: Ship as prison, making another connection to *Great Expectations* where the convict Magwitch is kept in a hulk. "Hulks are prison-ships, right 'cross th' meshes" (chapter 2).

4. Triskele

The next winter, Severian wanders into a lost part of the citadel searching for his dog Triskele and meets a young woman named Valeria near the Atrium of Time.

Apollo: The word "triskele" is Greek meaning "three legs." John Clute pointed out that the word in classical times "designated a three-legged icon used in the worship of Apollo" (*Strokes*, 151). The Greek god Apollo, god of the Sun, has other lesser-known aspects including wolves and disease.

Dickens: Valeria seems like the rich-girl Estella, Pip's bride-to-be, first seen in chapter 8 of *Great Expectations*.

Estella, as yet unnamed, guides Pip toward the place she calls Manor House

"Is that the name of this house, miss?"
  "One of its names, boy."
  "It has more than one, miss?"
  "One more. Its other name was Satis; which is Greek, or Latin, or Hebew, or all three—or all one to me—for enough."
  "Enough House," said I; "that's a curious name, miss."

Estella leads him to a strange interview with Miss Havisham, the mistress of the house, after a few pages of which Pip notes:

It was then I began to understand that everything in the room had stopped, like the watch and the clock, a long time ago. I noticed that Miss Havisham put down the jewel exactly on the spot from which she had taken it up. As Estella dealt the cards, I glanced at the dressing-table again, and saw that the shoe upon it, once white, now yellow, had never been worn. I glanced down at the foot from which the shoe was absent, and saw that the silk stocking on it, once white, now yellow, had been trodden ragged. Without this arrest of everything, this standing still of all the pale decayed objects, not even the withered bridal dress on the collapsed form could have looked so like grave-clothes, or the long veil so like a shroud.

A place of halted time, a place's name, and dead languages all figure in this exchange between Severian and Valeria:

"Is that what you call it? The Atrium of Time? Because of the dials, I suppose."
  "No, the dials were put there because we call it that. Do you like the dead languages? They have mottos. '*Lux dei vitae viam monstrat,*' that's 'The beam of the New Sun lights the way of life.' '*Felicibus brevis, miseris hora longa.*' 'Men wait long for happiness.' '*Aspice ut aspiciar.*'"
  I had to tell her with some shame that I knew no tongue beyond the one we spoke, and little of that. (44-45)

Shakespeare: The line Valeria utters, "I am all the sisters we breed. And all the sons" (45), connects her to Shakespeare's Viola, who says in *Twelfth Night,* "I am all the daughters of my father's house, And all the brothers too" (Act II, scene 4, line 118). Greg Feeley sharps the Shakespeare shaping in 1991 (*New York Review of Science Fiction No. 32,* p. 13).
  Rose: Roses in the Atrium of Time (43).

5. The Picture-Cleaner and Others

Severian becomes captain of the apprentices. On an errand, he meets Rudesind the curator. The picture he is cleaning shows an astronaut on the Moon. Rudesind gives Severian directions to the Library.

Americana: The Astronaut on the Moon picture (49) of 1969.

Apollo: Historically the astronaut of the picture was in the Apollo Program.

Animal Form: Rudesind as turtle (50).

Mervyn Peake: Rudesind the curator of the pinakotheken (51) finds a parallel in Rottcodd the curator in the Hall of Bright Carvings of *Titus Groan* (1945) by Mervyn Peake. Rottcodd, unmarried, dusts the carvings every day. Note the similarity of the names.

C. N. Manlove in 1986 notes a general influence of Peake at work in *The Book of the New Sun* (*Science Fiction: Ten Explorations,* p. 198). Wolfe, during an interview with Robert Frazier, says, "You didn't mention Peake's Gormenghast series, but . . . I suspect *The Book of the New Sun* is more like them than it is like [C. S.] Lewis' work, or Tolkien's" (Wright's *Shadows of the New Sun,* p. 53).

Wolfe expounds upon the Gormenghast trilogy in his interview with Malcolm Edwards (Wright's *Shadows of the New Sun,* 17-18).

6. The Master of the Curators

At the Library of Nessus Severian meets Master Ultan and apprentice Cyby. Ultan quotes phrases from books. Severian gets four books (one of them is brown, one is green) requested by an exultant prisoner.

Plato: When Ultan says, "It is unwise to know too much about these practices [involving the eating of the dead] . . . though when I think of sharing the mind of a historian like Loman, or Hermas" (52), he speaks like Socrates: "What would not a man give if he might converse with Orpheus and Musaeus and Hesiod and Homer?" (Plato's *Apology,* 40B).

Bible: Ultan's line "Of the trail of ink there is no end" (59) seems to draw from Ecclesiastes "of making many books there is no end; and much study wearies the body" (Ecclesiastes 12:12).

Boswell: Ultan's observation "A man will give his life to the turning over of a collection of books" (59) appears related to a quote from Boswell's *Life of Samuel Johnson* (1791), from April 6, 1775: "A man will turn over half a library to make one book." This phrase from Dr. Johnson is alluded to by Gene Wolfe in the article "Books in *The Book of the New Sun*" (Wright's *Shadows of the New Sun,* 195), but he does not state the connection with Ultan's statement.

Language of Flowers: Ultan recalls rosemary (60), and rosemary means "remembrance."

Shakespeare: Ultan tells of a library inside of a gem so small "a harlot might dangle it from one ear" (61), which seems close to Romeo's first sight of Juliet: "It seems she hangs upon the cheek of night As a rich jewel in an Ethiope's ear" (Act I, scene 5, lines 43-5).

Borges: Ultan's line, "He who had given all books into my keeping made me blind so that I should know in whose keeping the keepers stand" (61) draws from the opening of "Poem about Gifts" (1959) by Borges:

> Let none think I by tear or reproach make light
> Of this manifesting the mastery
> Of God, who with excellent irony
> Gives me at once both books and night.

The character Ultan is based on Borges himself, who became director of the National Public Library in Argentina, only to become blind shortly thereafter.

There is a notion that Ultan's assistant Cybe is based on Norman Thomas di Giovanni (1933-2017), who translated many books by Borges, beginning with *The Book of Imaginary Beings* (1957). Brought to my attention by Dan Parmenter (Urth List 26 AUG 1998).

Also noteworthy to this chapter, the Borges story "The Library of Babel" (1941) describes a vast library.

The Book of Gold: The librarians use this tome to recruit new members (62). In the following passage, Wolfe alludes to the single title that was his personal *Book of Gold*:

> There was a time when I could put the palm of my hand flat on the front of a tattered paperback called *The Dying Earth* and feel the magic seeping through the cardboard: Turjan of Miir, Liane the Wayfarer, T'sais, Chun the Unavoidable. Nobody I knew had so much as heard of that book, but I knew it was the finest book in the world. (*Castle of Days*, 211)

Enamel: The green book has enameled pictures of holy scenes (67). This subject is being tracked because of a thread in Wolfe's article "Books in *The Book of the New Sun*," which provocatively says that we might learn from tracking "enamel" in the text (Wright's *Shadows of the New Sun*, 197).

7. The Traitress

Severian meets Thecla, the prisoner who requested the books, and learns from Master Gurloes that she is being held as a lever against Vodalus, since her half-sister Thea is Vodalus's lover.

Wolf: Thecla as dire wolf (70).

Proust/history: The word "bordereau" (78) was once heavy with associations of corruption and betrayal:

Linked to the infamous Dreyfus treason case that convulsed France for a decade (1894-1904), "bordereau" was internationally understood as meaning one thing only: the key document of the case, the secret plans that were allegedly drawn up by Dreyfus. (*Lexicon Urthus*)

(Tip of the hat to David Langford for this point.)

8. The Conversationalist

Severian is assigned to keep Thecla company, but to guard against infatuation with a prisoner, he is sent to a brothel in the Algedonic Quarter.

Proust: The scenario here finds a surprising connection to *The Captive* (1923), the fifth volume of Marcel Proust's *Remembrance of Things Past,* in which the narrator keeps his lover Albertine as a virtual prisoner. He torturers himself psychologically over her, alternates between trying to please her and trying to leave her.

In his 1981 interview with Joan Gordon, Wolfe includes Proust in a list of authors he admires (Wright's *Shadows of the New Sun,* 27). In his 1988 interview with Larry McCaffrey, Wolfe says, "Proust, of course, was obsessed with some of the same things I deal with in *The Book of the New Sun*—memory and the way memory affects us—except that he was writing his remarkable works eighty years before I was" (ibid, 87). In his 1992 interview with James B. Jordan, Wolfe declares, "I am a great Proust fan. I have read *Remembrance of Things Past* I think about two and a half times. I don't read it more because when I start reading it I stop reading everything else" (ibid, 115).

9. The House Azure

At the brothel, Severian hires a woman who calls herself Thecla.

Bible: Stained glass insert showing the Temptation (88), alluding to Genesis 3:1-5.

Proust: In the first volume of *Remembrance of Things Past,* the narrator as a boy develops a crush for the Duchess de Guermantes, an infatuation which grows from a variety of signs and symbols, including her ancient lineage, a famed tapestry, a tomb effigy, and a stained-glass window. At one point he dreams that the duchess falls in love with him and they fish trout all day. Later, when he meets the actual woman, he is aware of the difference between image and reality; and, later still, he has real girlfriends, first Albertine and then Gilberte.

In a similar fashion, Severian first sees Thea in the graveyard (chapter 1), then he meets her half-sister Thecla as a prisoner (chapter 7). He has thoughts on their ancient lineage, then he is sent to a brothel where he meets a false Thecla, along with a false Thea.

Burning Rose: Thecla's perfume scent is rose burning (91).

10. The Last Year

Despite all the precautions, Severian falls in love with the prisoner Thecla.

Rose: First the dark death roses, purple flecked with scarlet (99). Next, Thecla's line "Here Rose the Graced . . ." (99) comes from the tomb of Fair Rosamond, a.k.a. Rosamond Clifford, concubine of Henry II (1133-89). Wolfe gives this version of her death:

> Those lines were originally applied to the Fayre Rosamund (Rosamund means *rose of the world*), the mistress of Henry II of England. Henry built a maze to hide her, but one day Queen Eleanor came with her knights and surprised Rosamund while she was embroidering . . . . She fled into the maze; but she dropped her needlework as she ran, and the ball of thread remained in the pocket of her gown. The queen's knights followed the thread and killed her. She died in 1175. (*Castle of Days,* 231-32)

Language of Flowers: Lilies purple-striped and white-dotted (96). Lily has many meanings, depending upon the type: Day Lily means Coquetry; Imperial Lily means Majesty; White Lily means Purity, Sweetness; Yellow Lily means Falsehood, Gaiety.

11. The Feast

Severian is elevated to journeyman and has another dream-vision.

Dubious Saint: The legend of Holy Katharine (106-8) recited by the torturers is like that of Saint Catherine of Alexandria, even to the detail that she was condemned by a ruler named "Maxentius" (106). Wolfe writes on Catherine of Alexandria: "She protested Maxentius's treatment of Christians, and was sentenced to die . . . on a spiked wheel. It broke . . . and she was decapitated instead. Legend has it that the wheel not only broke, but broke out in roses; the firework called a catherine wheel commemorates their blazing reds, yellows, and whites" (*Castle of Days,* 213-14).

Saint Catherine of Alexandria was very popular for a thousand years, yet modern times found her to be a dubious saint. In 1969 the Roman Catholic Church removed her feast day from the General Roman Calendar.

Burning Rose: Roses erupt from the Wheel of Holy Katharine (107), symbols of flame.

Visionary Experience: Severian has an episode that mixes many elements, including Thecla's perfume (109) and a visit by Malrubius (110).

12. The Traitor

Two days later the torture of Thecla begins, and Severian breaks the law by giving her a knife with which to kill herself.

Kafka: The apparatus (115) is a torture machine from Kafka's story "In the Penal Colony" (1919).

13. The Lictor of Thrax

For his crime against the guild, Severian is ordered to become the Lictor of Thrax, a distant provincial capital to which he must walk.

14. *Terminus Est*

As a parting gift Master Palaemon gives him the sword *Terminus Est,* and Severian also takes the brown book. His presence on the bridge causes a disturbance, so he is interviewed by a lochage.

Cryptic Cross: "And so I trudged along . . . a somberly clad traveler who shouldered a dark patrissa" (I, chap. 14, 131), where a patrissa is a staff topped by a cross, a crosier.

Henry Mayhew: An eccentric exultant named Talarican is paraphrased by the lochage of the bridge in his talk with Severian (134). From *Lexicon Urthus:* "David Langford reports that Talarican's statistical interest seems akin to journalist Henry Mayhew's *London Labor and the London Poor* (1851)."

15. Baldanders

After crossing the bridge into the living city, Severian is in need of lodging. He shares a bed with the giant Baldanders. He has a vision-dream of undines and puppets. In the morning he meets Doctor Talos.

Borges: Baldanders has an entry in *The Book of Imaginary Beings.* Borges says the character comes from *The Adventurous Simplicissimus Teutch* (1669) by Johann Hans Jakob Cristoffel von Grimmelshausen.

Melville: The "share a room"/"share a bed" sequence (137-39) shows a tie to *Moby Dick* (1851), specifically chapters 3 and 4, where the narrator Ishmael hears about the absent cannibal Queequeg, then shares his bed with a weapon between them.

Vision Dream: Severian's vision-dream has three scenes. In the first Severian rides on a flying creature (139-40); the second has Severian touring underwater (140-41); and the third is a toy puppet play (141-42).

Pinocchio: "Talos" is a figure from Greek myth, but Doctor Talos (142) seems more like the Fox from *Pinocchio* (1883). That is, Doctor Talos has a fox face; he is a member of a two-man team; this team has a connection to theater. All point to the Fox and Cat characters in *Pinocchio.* In the Disney version (1940) they persuade Pinocchio to join Stromboli's puppet show.

Animal Form: Talos as thrush (143).

16. The Rag Shop

At a breakfast cafe Talos tries to convince Severian to travel with them and act in their play, but Severian decides to skip their planned meeting at Ctesiphon's Cross and goes to buy clothes at a rag shop.

Ctesiphon's Cross: Dr. Talos says, "Severian, we will perform, I think, at Ctesiphon's Cross" (149). Initially this place name seems to denote a location possessing a crucifix monument. But historically the Islamic city Ctesiphon received the True Cross as plunder after the Sassanian conquest of Byzantine Jerusalem in AD 614. Following this, "Ctesiphon's Cross" might be another name for the True Cross.

James Joyce: Surveying the city he walks through, Severian lists various types of buildings, including "artellos" (150), a typo for "martellos" (*Castle of Days*, 241). Martellos are simple towers, but one near Dublin is most famous because it sheltered a major character at the beginning of the novel *Ulysses* (1922).

Dickens: The rag shop associated within the work of Charles Dickens is found in chapter five of *Bleak House* (1853) and there is some evidence that Dickens was influenced by Mayhew's work *London Labour and the London Poor* (1851). (Mayhew's book was referenced in notes to chapter 14: *Terminus Est.*)

Entering the rag shop, Severian is startled to see a man who seemed "a corpse left erect behind the counter in fulfillment of the morbid wish of some past owner" (153). This Dickensian detail finds historical trace to Bentham's "auto-icon," the remains of Jeremy Bentham (1748-1832) kept on public display at University College London since 1850.

Animal Form: Agia's pavonine gown (152) associates her with the peacock.

Apollo: The above-mentioned peacock is a well-known symbol of Hera, Queen of the Gods. This is a danger sign, since Hera tried to kill the young Apollo, a "new son" of her philandering husband Zeus and the Titaness Leto.

17. The Challenge

Agilus, the shopkeeper of the rag shop, tries hard to talk Severian into selling *Terminus Est* to him, but Severian refuses; suddenly, an officer of the Septentrions enters the shop and wordlessly delivers a challenge to mortal combat with averns on the Sanguinary Field.

Bible: "Sanguinary Field" (157) seems close to "Akeldama" (Aramaic "field of blood"), a place in Jerusalem associated in the Bible with Judas Iscariot, the apostle who betrayed Jesus (Acts 1: 18-19; Matthew 27:7).

Animal Form: The Septentrion (157) is named after a bear, from the Great Bear constellation.

John Bunyan: Severian writes, "So I became, in appearance at least, a pilgrim bound for some vague northern shrine. Have I said that time turns our lies into truths?" (I, chap. 17, 160). This detail puts into play *The Pilgrim's Progress* (1678), considered by some to be the first novel in English.

Bunyan and his most famous work are not mentioned in lists offered by Gene Wolfe in interviews. Well, not accurately: in Frazier's 1983 interview, Wolfe is talking about the works of C. S. Lewis and "Pilgrim's Progress" is mentioned where *Pilgrim's Regress* (1933), an early novel by Lewis, is clearly intended (Wright's *Shadows of the New Sun*, 52).

Wolfe does mention the author and his book in the essay "From a House on the Borderland." In writing about the sudden growth of literacy that was justified by religion, he states: "Reading the Bible was all right—very much so. Reading a book like *Pilgrim's Progress* was probably okay too" (*Castle of Days*, 410), and later, "Those long-dead men and women who learned to read so that they might read the Bible and John Bunyan would tell us that pride is the greatest of all sins, the father of sin. And the victims of the new illiteracy are proud of it" (412).

18. The Destruction of the Altar

Agia, twin sister of Agilus, agrees to help Severian prepare for the duel, but then she involves them in a cab race. Their cab plows into a giant tent, destroying the alter of the Pelerines and thereby losing the Claw of the Conciliator, a holy gem.

Wolf: Agia as thylacine (162), the marsupial wolf.

Little Red Riding Hood: Inside the cathedral tent, Severian sees "a cluster of scarlet-clad people . . . . a woman . . . wore a hood and narrow cape that trailed long tassels" (167). This is Severian's first glimpse of the little red riding hood.

Robert van Gulik: The "scarlet pelerine" is a signature feature in the "Judge Dee" novels of van Gulik, mysteries set in seventh-century China. In *Celebrated Cases of Judge Dee* (Dover edition), at chapter 30 Judge Dee has solved the cases and is preparing for the administering of penalties, for which phase he dons a scarlet pelerine (p. 213). In the Chinese legal system of the Tang dynasty a scarlet pelerine is a symbol of severity, which is fitting since the penalties involve torture and death.

During Wolfe's 1981 interview with Joan Gordon he lists van Gulik among authors he admires (Wright's *Shadows of the New Sun*, p. 27).

19. The Botanic Gardens

Agia tells Severian something about the Pelerines as they continue on foot to the Botanic Gardens to select an avern flower for the duel. At the Gardens they become sidetracked by a visit to the Sand Garden. At one point in her banter, Agia says, "Urvasi loved Pururavas, you know, before she saw him in a bright light."

Pelerines: In the previous chapter Agia had mentioned that the Pelerines are "a band of priestesses who travel the continent" (chap. 18, 167). Their very large tent is made of silk (chap. 18, 169), and looking back at it, Severian terms it a tent-cathedral (chap. 19, 170). Agia continues her telling, calling the Pelerines "professional virgins" (170) who temporarily seize land, raise money, and move on. All this gives the impression that they are like the tent revival groups that moved across the United States beginning in the 1800s.

Myth: In Hindu mythology, Urvasi (172) was the most famous of the Apsaras ("daughters of pleasure"), spirits renowned for wantonness. She once consented to live with Pururavas, a human king, but she told him that human nakedness disgusted her. He promised she would never have to see him unclothed, but then he forgot one day, and she fled. Only when he promised to leave his throne and become an erotic singer-dancer did she agree to return.

Contrarian Severian: The curator urges them to visit the Garden of Antiquities (176), and Agia recommends the Garden of Delectation (177), but Severian selects the Sand Garden.

Language of Flowers: Lianas (178).

20. Father Inire's Mirrors

Severian and Agia go on a side trip to the Jungle Garden, where Severian tells a story of little girls and Father Inire's magic mirrors.

Language of Flowers: Thecla's hands like white lilies (181), and White Lily means Purity, Sweetness.

Myth: The fauna of mirrors is a Chinese notion that goes back to the legendary times of the Yellow Emperor.

Borges: "The first to awaken will be the Fish" ("Fauna of Mirrors" entry in *The Book of Imaginary Beings*).

21. The Hut in the Jungle

Severian and Agia visit a missionary hut in the jungle. Agia tells him if he avoids the duel, assassins will come after him with the yellow beard snake.

Bible: The woman reading the Bible (181) is quoting Deuteronomy 34:1-6, about the death of Moses.

Geography: The place seems to be in tropical Africa, because the name "Isangoma" is a Zulu title for a diviner.

20th Century: The mail plane (191-92) Severian sees seems to be an artifact from the 20th century.

Rex Stout: Agia tells Severian that if he avoids the duel, assassins will come after him with "the snake called yellowbeard" (192). Since the other name for that South American viper is "fer-de-lance," this might be an encrypted allusion to Stout's *Fer-de-Lance* (1934), the first of the Nero Wolfe mysteries.

For one thing, in that novel the criminal tries to assassinate the detective with a deadly fer-de-lance hidden in a desk.

In notes on his short story "The Rubber Bend" (1974), Wolfe writes that it "brings in—as a robot—my favorite private eye, Nero Wolfe" (Introduction to *Storeys From the Old Hotel*).

Art Studies: The missionary Robert, describing his "vision" of Severian and Agia, mentions "Death and the Lady" (190), a reference to the art motif "Death and the Maiden," which was common in Renaissance art and revived during the Romantic era. Note that Robert does not call Agia a maiden.

Commentary: The missionaries Robert and Marie seem like 20th century people trapped in a semi-fantastic place. I have a suspicion that "Robert" is actually Robert W. Chambers (1865-1933), a blending of his life and his signature fictions.

Chambers left his hometown of Brooklyn to study art in Paris from 1886 to 1893. His illustrations were commercially successful but beginning in 1887 he turned to writing, *The King in Yellow* (1895) being his most famous work today.

Chambers often wrote fictions of a hunter encountering fey women in the woods. "The Maker of Moons" (1896) is a good example, where in the end of a weird adventure tale we get a note that Ysonde, the fey woman now a dream wife, asks him to quit writing for the day—suggesting that the whole is a mere fantasy, or that the hunter has not come back from that world. Then there is "The Demoiselle D'Ys" of *The King in Yellow,* where the fey woman warns the hunter of his return trip: "to come is easy and takes hours; to go is different—and may take centuries." This line by itself seems to capture the time-bending aspect of the jungle path that Severian and Agia are on.

22. Dorcas

Severian and Agia enter the Garden of Everlasting Sleep, which is both a park and an aquatic cemetery. They meet an old boatman searching for his long dead wife "Cas." His boat is too small to ferry them. Severian loses *Terminus Est* in the Lake of Birds and dives after it.

Commentary: Severian says he first thought of the averns growing in a conservatory, then that the Botanic Gardens would be like the necropolis (195). Even so, in a few paragraphs he learns the Garden of Everlasting Sleep is a cemetery.

Geography: The place seems to be near Naples, Italy.

Dante: When the unnamed boatman says, "Too heavy for my little boat" (196) he seems to echo Charon of Dante's *Inferno:*

"And thou, who there
Standest, live spirit! get thee hence, and leave
These who are dead." But soon as he beheld

I left them not, "By other way," said he,
"By other haven shalt thou come to shore,
Not by this passage; thee a nimbler boat
Must carry." (canto 3, lines 79-90)

Which draws from Virgil's *Aeneid* (book 6, lines 298-304; 384-416).

In both cases the ferryman initially refuses to take a living man on his boat.

Bog Bodies: When the boatman says "The water here pickles them" (198), the link is made to bog bodies, human corpses naturally mummified in a peat bog. The cadavers are preserved by the acidic water, low temperature, and lack of oxygen. Bog bodies from the Iron Age show signs of violent death and lack of clothing, suggesting either human sacrifice or the execution of criminals. These dark associations are of high contrast to an aquatic cemetery.

Enamel: Cloisonné (199).

King Arthur: The lake, the lady, the sword—this tableau comes from the Arthurian Cycle (*Gene Wolfe: 14 Articles on His Fiction,* 27-28).

23. Hildegrin

Severian is helped out of the water by Dorcas, a young woman with amnesia, and the three of them are ferried across the lake by Hildegrin the Badger, a man Severian recognizes as the grave-digging henchman of Vodalus.

Cryptic Cross: "Rood" (204), an archaic term used to describe a crucifix, here denoting crucifixes at Dorcas's cloisonné shop (noted in Greg Feeley's essay in *The New York Review of Science Fiction No. 31,* p.10). Add to a new category with Ctesiphon's Cross.

Dante: When Severian gathers his wits, it is almost as if he too is on a different shore—in addition to Agia, there is the nameless blonde woman (Dorcas) who helped him out of the water, and there is also "a big, beef-faced man" (who will turn out to be Hildegrin). "Beef-faced man" sounds like an allusion to the Minotaur, another figure of Greek mythology who also appears in Dante's *Inferno,* as the first guardian of the Seventh Circle of Hell. One of the first things that Hildegrin says is "Who in Phlegethon are you?" and Phelegethon is the fiery river of blood which flows through the Seventh Circle, that region reserved for those who committed violence against others. (*Gene Wolfe: 14 Articles,* 29)

Myth: To help the wet and shivering couple, Hildegrin offers them brandy from a flask in the shape of a dog with the bone in his mouth as the stopper— a reference to the sop for Cerberus, the guardian of Hades who appears in many tales of the underworld. . . .

That Dorcas cannot at first remember her own name points to Lethe— she has drunk of the waters of forgetfulness. (ibid, 29)

Robert Graves: When Hildegrin points out to them the Cave of the

Cumaean (208), this links to the opening of *I, Claudius,* where Emperor Claudius visits the Cumaean sibyl.

Commentary: On the head-spinning transition from chapter 22 to chapter 23, being Severian's odd experience in the Lake of Birds. First noting the quality of the water, "laced and thickened with the fibrous stems of the reeds" (201); the depth of his descent, "As it was, eight or ten cubits [twelve to fifteen feet] beneath the surface"; his sense that the hand is "drawing me down."

The new chapter begins with Dorcas helping Severian out of the water. The implication seems to be that Severian had a recurrence of the disorientation he had experienced in his previous near-drowning experience, and in comparing the two, we see the similarity of the aquatic roots and stems in both cases, but also the lack of a death vision in the lake episode.

To review, Severian ran to catch up with Agia (chap. 22, 200). When he was about to overtake her, he accidentally slipped into the water. Realizing he had dropped the sword, he dove down after it. His one hand found the sword and his other found a hand that pulled him down. End of chapter.

Severian, near exhaustion, throws his sword up onto the sedge (chap. 23, 202). Someone takes him by the wrist. He expects it to be Agia, but it is a teenage blonde. He rests there for a minute or two ("as long as it takes to say the angelus"), then Agia and Hildegrin arrive.

Agia looks pale with fright. Hildegrin asks where the blonde teen came from. Agia says she looked back to see what was distracting Severian, and saw the blonde was pulling him onto the sedge. This is rendered paradoxical to Severian's account both in time and space: he was about to overtake Agia, about to offer his arm, which sounds so close we might expect her to be splashed when he tumbled into the water. Yet by her version, Agia was a minute or two away, and when she looked back the blonde was already helping him out of the water (203). For his part, Hildegrin says he only came over because he saw a man drowning (205). So Agia and Hildegrin were about the same distance away from the spot.

24. The Flower of Dissolution

Severian picks the avern flower before leaving the garden with Dorcas and Agia.

Chapter Title: "The Flower of Dissolution" suggests the lotus of Buddha and the illusion of reality called the veil of maya. Yet the first sentence has Dorcas drawing a hyacinth from the lake as if by magic, causing Severian to wonder "Is it possible the flower came into being only because Dorcas reached for it?" That the flower "materializes" stands in stark opposition to the "dissolution" of the chapter title. (*Gene Wolfe: 14 Articles,* 30-31)

Language of Flowers: Dorcas wears the water hyacinth, a flower that means "constancy." Traced by Roy C. Lackey.

Proust: In true Proustian style, the observation of this simple act (a young woman plucking a flower from the water) sets off in Severian a meditation on opposites, the nature of light and darkness, and the illusion of reality. Such thoughts add to the Buddhistic mood. (*Gene Wolfe: 14 Articles,* 31)

King Arthur: Crossing the misty waters, heading for the farther shore of Avalon— this is the "Death of Arthur" scene, the dissolution of Logres. With Dorcas as the Lady of the Lake, Hildegrin as Morgan le Fay, and Agia as the Lady of Avalon. (ibid, 31)

The Aeneid: When Severian actually picks his avern we see Aeneas plucking the Golden Bough of Proserpina (a key to the underworld) at the beginning of his otherworld quest. (ibid, 31)

Commentary: Dorcas is a "little sister" character who takes on the role of moral guide, like the cricket in Disney's *Pinoccio.* Even so, her teaching method is sometimes rather immoral.

25. The Inn of Lost Loves

Severian, Agia, and Dorcas make reservations for dinner at a tree-house restaurant, staying for a snack.

Mervyn Peake: Abban the master of the inn (219) is similar to Abiatha Swelter, the chef of Gormenghast, introduced in the chapter "Swelter" of *Titus Groan* (1946). Abiatha is monstrously fat, a drunkard, and a bully. He has a long running fight with another staff member that leads to attempted murder by cleaver. Note the similarity in names, seen before with Rudesind and Rottcudd. (See notes for chapter 5: The Picture Cleaner and Others.)

Our innkeeper Abban is sinister in that he has assisted in Agia's murderous game before (220).

Language of Wine: Medoc (220; 222).

Rose: When Agia quips "the rose hath stabbed the iris" (223), she equates the avern with a white rose and herself with an iris.

Language of Flowers: "Iris" equals "message"; "white rose" means "I am worthy of you."

Bible: Treehouse restaurant and the crucifixion. Since it is a common metaphor to refer to the cross as a tree, and since this is the last stop before Sanguinary Field (which might be Akeldama), there is a suggestion that Severian's going up into the tree is a reference to the crucifixion.

26. Sennet

Severian gets involved in a little intrigue with the staff, then it is time for the duel.

Agia's Vocabulary Fails: When Agia tells Severian about the

"machionations" of the city wall, she apparently fumbles the real word "machicolations" (being a type of "downspouts"), rather than using the more expected "merlons" or "crenels" (being respectively the notches and highpoints in a battlement). Earlier in her banter about the Conciliator, she said "thirty thousand years ago" (I, chap. 19, 172) and thus, in hindsight we see she avoided the more educated term "chiliad," which itself might serve as a marker of social status.

Cryptic Crosier: The avern mounted on a pole is carried by Agia like a baculus (I, chap. 26, 233), where a baculus is the pastoral staff of a bishop, shaped like a shepherd's staff.

27. Is He Dead?

At the duel Severian is treacherously struck dead, but he rises up and his opponent panics, killing spectators in his attempt to flee.

Commentary: "The world was a great paschal egg, crowded with all the colors of the palette" (239). An Easter Egg, where Easter celebrates a resurrection.

28. Carnifex

Severian wakes up the next morning in the lazaret of the Blue Dimarchi, and learns that he must execute his former opponent.

Robert Graves: Dorcas says the avern has "the face poison would have" (244), a line similar to something Claudius wrote: "I once saw a strange painting on the inside of an old chest . . . The inscription . . . was 'Poison is Queen,' and the face of Poison, though executed over a hundred years before Livia's birth, was unmistakably the face of Livia" (I, Claudius, chap. 3, paragraph 2).

Rex Stout: When Dorcas says the avern itself strikes like a snake (245), she pays out on the Fer-de-Lance hint given by Agia before. In Stout's novel, the first mystery is a death on a golf course, which involves an elaborate device treacherously killing an unsuspecting victim with poison on an open green field. I believe the duel with averns is a translation of that golf game gambit.

Commentary: Dorcas was aided in dealing with the avern when "a woman who had been fighting somewhere else came with a braquemar" (245), a short sword. This is probably "Laurentia of the House of the Harp," one of the three names being called out.

29. Agilus

The former opponent turns out to be Agilus.

Talmud: When Agilus is trying to talk his way out of prison, he says

Severian has wronged him three times, and that by "the old law" (253) he thus owes Agilus a boon.

Research reveals this is a twisted and distorted detail from the Jewish Talmud, where, as part of the preparation for year's end, one seeks forgiveness from a friend one has wronged three times, and if he does not forgive you, the sin is no longer your own.

In the Talmud it is about forgiveness, not about a "get out of jail" card.

Myth: Agia had left a scratched image on the stones that "might have been the snarling face of Jurupari" (255). Jurupari was the chief god of the Uapes tribe of Brazil. His cult was associated with male initiation rites from which women were excluded, under punishment of death by poison.

Jack Vance: Agia revealed as a femme fatale exposes her similarity to T'sais, the beautiful yet twisted woman in a couple of stories ("Turjan of Miir" and "T'sais") in *The Dying Earth*. Turjan, while searching for the sorcerer Pandelume who might teach him a spell, encounters T'sais, who immediately attacks him.

Commentary: Revealing that the combat (of chapter 27) was rigged, in that the warmth of Severian's hands would stimulate the avern and it would strike at his face (253). This makes it seem probable that Agia's "machionations" flub in chapter 26 was a Freudian Slip for "machination," since the evil twins clearly had a secret plot against Severian. But for their motive, Agia and Agilus tell Severian that they were driven to murder him by the treasure of his sword (252).

30. Night

The night before the execution, Severian meets Hethor, an old sailor.

Language of Flowers: During the day Dorcas wears a daisy, which, if white means "innocence," but if wild means "I will think of it." In the evening Dorcas wears a moonflower, which means "attachment; I attach myself to you." (Nod to Roy C. Lackey.)

Hethor tells of his shipboard sex doll, which had irises "purple like asters or pansies" (257), where aster means "variety" and pansy means "thoughts."

Jack Vance: That Severian has carnal knowledge of his moral tutor seems like something Cugel would do. While the rogue Cugel first appeared in *The Eyes of the Overworld* (1966), the episode "The Seventeen Virgins" (1974), collected in *Cugel's Saga* (1983), is closer to the topic.

Pinocchio: Then again, the original Pinocchio killed the Talking Cricket, who nevertheless continued to advise him as a ghost.

Triskele: A Triskele memory (261).

31. The Shadow of the Torturer

After the execution, while Severian and Dorcas are walking towards the gate of Nessus, Severian suddenly discovers he has been carrying the Claw of the Conciliator (planted on him by Agia after the crash), and they see the miracle of the flying cathedral.

Myth: That Severian has a "magic" sword and a sacred gem is a pattern similar to the Three Sacred Treasures of Japan (a sword, a mirror, and a jewel). These three items are related to the sun goddess Amaterasu, and her sacred jewel has a curious, comma shape.

Claw Notes: The gem is coin shaped (268), rather than spherical.

Commentary: Severian belatedly realizes that Agia was hoping to retrieve the Claw after his death, in addition to the sword (269).

32. The Play

By accident they meet Doctor Talos's dramatic troupe just in time to act in the play. Talos calls Severian "Death" and Dorcas "Innocence."

Language of Trees: Beech (273) symbolizes prosperity.

Language of Flowers: Talos calling Dorcas "Innocence" reinforces the white daisy reading of chapter 30.

Commentary: While Talos had said in chapter 16 that the play would be performed at Ctesiphon's Cross, in chapter 32 the text gives no assurance, showing no evidence of a monument. In fact, Talos's estimation of Ctesiphon's Cross as a venue was for a night some days earlier, leading some readers to reasonably presume that is where Talos and Baldanders performed on their first night with Jolenta.

33. Five Legs

Severian has a dream-vision involving the ghosts of Master Malrubius and Severian's dog, Triskele.

Jack Vance: When Talos decapitates flowers with his cane (279) he exhibits a trait shared with T'sais, the femme fatale in two stories of *The Dying Earth*.

Thematic Echo: The line in the center of the Claw is like a "scimitar blade" (280), a link to the scimitars carried by the men in the Cathedral of the Claw (chap. 18, 167).

Frame Tale: Severian addresses the reader directly, "You, who will some day delve in Master Ultan's library" (281), revealing how he supposes his book will be read.

Commentary: The appearance of ghostly forms of Malrubius and Triskele is curious because while Malrubius is known to be dead, Triskele is presumably still alive. Looking back in the text of chapter 4, Severian saw Triskele again for the first time about a week after he lost him (45-46), and then once or twice a month "for as long as the snow lasted" (46).

34. Morning

Severian learns the actress's name is Jolenta.

Thematic Echo: Jolenta swallows a grape whole (287), thematic echo to Thecla swallowing a leek (chap. 7, 72).

Bible: "'Red as the apples of . . .' I can't think of it. Would you like a bite?" (288). The word Dorcas cannot recall is probably "Eden."

35. Hethor

The party meets a sailor named Jonas who says the Pelerines went north out the Gate of Nessus. As they enter the deep Piteous Gate, Talos frightens Jolenta and Dorcas with lurid speculation on the dwellers in the Wall. Jonas begins to tell them what he knows, but his story is cut off by a sudden riot.

Dickens: The character Jonas often uses Wellerisms (e.g. "I don't know what was wrong, but believe me, their departure was impressive and unmistakable—that's what the bear said, you know, about the picnickers," 297) like that of the character Sam Weller in *The Pickwick Papers* (1837). In 1991, Greg Feeley points out that Jonas speaks like Weller (*New York Review of Science Fiction No. 32*, p. 13).

Language of Trees: Oak (291).

Red: "[R]ed as pentecost" (292). The main sign of Pentecost in the West is the color red, symbolizing joy and the fire of the Holy Spirit.

Byzantine: The distressed Pelerines carry their deeses reversed (297). A deesis is a Byzantine icon showing Christ Pantocrator (alone) or Christ in Majesty (enthroned and attended by two or more figures). In this case the objects are portable icons, and they are being held upside down ("reversed").

Hieronymus Bosch: The strange soldiers inside the wall, with their "teeth like nails or hooks" (299), seem like a detail from the hallucinatory paintings of renaissance artist Hieronymus Bosch (1450-1516).

The Wall and Its Dwellers, or Jonas's Unfinished Story: Dr. Talos speaks of the Wall (299), which prompts an offer from Jonas to tell something about it. Talos makes one condition: "We will speak only of the Wall, and those who dwell in it." Accepting this rule, Jonas says,

> "In the old times, the lords of this world feared no one but their own people, and to defend themselves against them built a great fortress on a hilltop to the north of the city. I was not called Nessus then, for the river was unpoisoned.
>
> "Many of the people were angry at the building of that citadel, holding it their right to slay their lords without hindrance if they so desired. But others went out in the ships that ply between the stars, returning with treasure and knowledge. In time there returned a woman who had gained nothing among them but a handful of black

beans.

"She displayed the beans to the lords of men, and told them that unless she were obeyed she would cast them into the sea and so put an end to the world. They had her seized and torn to bits, for they were a hundred times more complete in their domination than our Autarch." (300-301)

At this point his tale is interrupted by the incident at the gate.

The story is fragmentary, yet we are assured that it relates to the Wall and its inhabitants, so the endpoint must be "this is why the Wall was built and this is what the dwellers are watching for."

Consider the hypothesis that the Wall was built because of the black beans and the world-ending threat they represent. The dwellers are watching for the black beans. They are protecting Urth, not Nessus; in fact the city might be destroyed in this task.

This solution fulfills the condition set by Dr. Talos. It also builds upon what Talos himself had just said, that the dwellers are watching for someone. It even lines up with Baldanders's claim that the Wall was not built for the expansion of Nessus (296). So in this reading, the likely thrust of Jonas's story is to dispel the sense of danger that Talos had created in Jolenta and Dorcas by assuring them that the dwellers are watching for a specific rare contraband, and that they are unlikely to spot it on this occasion since they have been watching for this substance since before the first autarch.

Jonas implies that citadel hill is the location of the singular port of Urth.

Myth: Jonas says the city back then was not called Nessus because it did not poison the river. This ties into the "Nessus as poisoner" aspect of Greek myth, brought up in notes for chapter 2.

Commentary: Severian killing the drover (301), an innocent man, ends the volume just as it had begun with his killing of the axman.

Appendix: A Note on the Translation

Gene Wolfe tells about his work at translating Severian's narrative.

Horace Walpole: Horatio Walpole, 4th Earl of Orford, invented the gothic novel with *The Castle of Otranto* (1764). This is an impressive work in many ways, with its blend of ancient and modern, but of key note here is that Walpole claimed to have translated it from medieval Italian, from a manuscript printed at Naples in 1529, based upon a story dating back to the Crusades. This ploy seems to have fooled some critics of the first edition.

VOLUME II: THE CLAW OF THE CONCILIATOR

But strength still goes out from your thorns,
    and from your abysses the sound of music.
Your shadows lie on my heart like roses
    and your nights are like strong wine.

Epigraph: *The Claw of the Conciliator* opens with a quotation, identified in *Castle of Days* as being from Gertrude von Le Fort ("Hands and Feet" article, page 229). More specifically, the lines are from her book *Hymns to the Church,* a collection of poems published in 1924 in Germany. In the 1944 English translation of the book, her name "Gertrud" is rendered with a final "E," as used by Wolfe.

The quote is the opening two lines from the fifth section of "Return to the Church," a poem in eight sections.

1. The Village of Saltus

Severian and Jonas are in the village of Saltus, about a week after the disturbance at the gate. They both want to meet up again with Doctor Talos's troupe, but Severian has to practice his art to earn money. Severian mentions that their water pitcher had wine in it. Severian learns he must execute Barnoch, a spy of Vodalus.

Bible: "Our water-ewer held wine" (8). This sentence alludes to the time Jesus turned water into wine at the wedding feast in Cana (John 2:1-11). It is counted as the first public miracle performed by Jesus.

Animal Form: Barnoch as a badger (10). This is curious since "badger" was already self-selected for Hildegrin (I, chap. 23).

Paradoxes to Perfect Memory: Mention of Vodalus (13) harkens to the scene with Vodalus giving away his pistol (I, chap. 1, 14-15), but this time the memory is semi-paradoxed by having Vodalus give it directly to Thea, rather than to Hildegrin, from whom Thea took it. As early as 1983 this detail is alluded to in *Realms of Fantasy* (p. 120) by Edwards and Holdstock as the first of two examples where Wolfe reveals problems in Severian's memory.

2. The Man in the Dark

As the spy is removed from his long-sealed house, Severian glimpses Agia.

Sophocles: Immurement as civic punishment is most famously found in the ancient Greek drama *Antigone* (441 BC), where the eponymous heroine is condemned to be sealed in a cave for the crime of providing funeral rites over her brother's corpse.

Echo: Inside the house, the sound of metal on stone (21) makes Severian recall when he hid the coin Vodalus had given him (I, chap. 3, 32).

Bible: Barnoch is a sort of reverse Lazarus. In part because of the badger connection established with tombs and tomb-robbing, perhaps.

3. The Showman's Tent

Trying to find Agia, Severian wanders into Saltus fair and meets the enslaved green man, a plant/man from the future. He leaves the slave a tool for escape.

Secret Santa: Cardamom-bread (22) is a common foodstuff in Scandinavia, but it is also famous as a traditional Christmas food.

John Bunyan: The Saltus fair episode evokes Vanity Fair of *The Pilgrim's Progress*. In Bunyan's book, the pilgrim Christian has many encounters on the road to the Celestial City. After passing through the Valley of the Shadow of Death he meets Faithful, another pilgrim, and together they have adventures before arriving at Vanity Fair.

In addition to the similarity of two recent friends arriving at a fair, there is also a point of congruence regarding executions: Vanity Fair's execution is incidental, but Saltus's are the reason for its fair, to capitalize upon the executions Severian will perform.

Echo: "Like the duelist who had called out" (23) is a link to the Sanguinary Field (I, chap. 27, 235).

Thematic Echo: The tent's "slight odor as of hay curing" (26) recalls the tent and the straw in the pelerine tent.

Surprising Religious Reaction: When the green man says that the day is brighter in his future age, Severian reports, "That simple remark thrilled me in a way that nothing had since I had first glimpsed the unroofed chapel in the Broken Court of our Citadel" (27).

This chapel is the one that the torturers feast in. First mentioned in chapter 5 as the "ruined chapel," it figures in his post-elevation dream/vision at the end of chapter 11.

Bible: The green man's future implies the New Sun arrival, even though he does not know of it. This makes him a sort of John the Baptist.

4. The Bouquet

Severian performs tortures and executions.

Roses: Threnodic roses, purple-black (35).

Mystery: This chapter is its own mystery tale. When Morwenna's husband Stachys and her son Chad died, she claimed it was from drinking bad water (32). Eusebia accused her of poisoning them. Morwenna was tried and found guilty. Through visiting her chained by the river's edge, where she is verbally tormented by the older woman Eusebia (32, 35), Severian deduces that Morwenna is greatly feared since she was not molested (32). After Severian has tortured and executed Morwenna, Eusebia exalts that her own revenge is complete: that she had killed Morwenna for stealing Stachys from her (38). The fact that Morwenna did not keep a dose of poison for herself proves to Eusebia that she was innocent of poisoning. Then Eusebia is poisoned by the perfume of her bouquet (39).

Onomastics: Looking to the names for clues turns up the curious detail that "Eusebia" is the name of a Roman Empress, the second wife of Constantius II. Her tenure on the Byzantine throne was from AD 353 to 360. She was childless and notorious for administering miscarriage-potions to others. While she supported Julian (who would become Julian the Apostate) as heir to the throne, Eusebia is supposed to have poisoned Julian's wife Helena: "[E]ven the fruits of [Julian's] marriage-bed were blasted by the jealous artifices of Eusebia herself" (Gibbon, *The Decline and Fall of the Roman Empire*, Volume 2, chapter 19). The elements of female jealousy, infertility, and use of poison are all there; Wolfe has rearranged things so that Morwenna (whose name means "maiden" in Welsh) is the poisoner rather than the victim.

5. The Bourne

Severian receives a secret note from Thecla, telling him that she is alive and waiting for him in a nearby mine. He goes there.

Chapter Title: A bourne is a small stream, especially one that flows intermittently or seasonally; but it is also a boundary, limit; goal, destination. Note that the text refers to "brook" in the letter Severian reads, and "brook" again when he encounters it. Within the mine it is "the stream."

Bible: "The better wine" (40), referring to the wine in the ewer, is a further allusion to the wine at the wedding feast in Cana. Specifically, the wedding guests noticed that this wine (created by Jesus) was superior to the wine they had been drinking before, which caused comment, because normally the best wine is served first.

6. Blue Light

At the mine Severian encounters the man-apes, guardians of the Autarch's treasure.

Dubious Saint: "I gulped air to shout *Thecla* once more. Then I knew, and closed my lips, and drew *Terminus Est*" (II, chap. 6, 51). Now is the proper time to mention that "The Acts of Paul and Thecla" is a book that was excluded from the Bible. The legend tells of how a virgin named Thecla heard Saint Paul preaching and committed her life to following Jesus. She shared a prison cell with Saint Paul and went through all sorts of trials with animals. Finally she ended up in a secure cave where she worked miracles of healing for seven decades until, to escape from approaching rapists, she was miraculously swallowed by the mountain.

The two details used by Wolfe are the sharing a prison cell and the disappearance within a mountain. The pattern for Saint Catherine of Alexandria holds true here as well: a once-popular saint declared dubious. In 1969 Thecla's cult was suppressed in the Roman Catholic Church.

Michael Crichton: The coming of the man-apes (49) shows similarities to a scene in Crichton's *Eaters of the Dead* (1976), wherein a narrator faces attack by a group of what turns out to be archaic human stock.

Severian in the mine, describing his first view of the strange light, writes:

[I]t was a luminous mist, sometimes seeming of no color, sometimes of an impure yellowish green. It was impossible to say how far it was, and it seemed to possess no shape . . . . Then it was joined by another. (49)

Three paragraphs later, the scene continues as more lights appear and collectively form shapes, then Severian hears a sound as the lights become more distinct:

Soon there were too many of the lights to count . . . I saw these flecks of light were coalescing into a pattern, and that the pattern was a dart or arrowhead pointed toward myself. Then I heard . . . a roaring. . . .
. . . . The roaring grew—not quite any noise of animals, yet not the shouting of the most frenzied human mob. I saw that the flecks of light were not shapeless . . . each was that figure called in art a star, having five unequal points. (49-50)

Three paragraphs later, the light resolve into human forms:

The stars were not sparks of light, but shapes like men . . . And the men, who seemed not men, being thicker of shoulder and more twisted than men, were rushing toward me. The roar I heard was the sound of their voices. (50-51)

Two paragraphs later, the non-human details become suddenly evident:

> They were terrible . . . like apes in that they had hairy, crooked bodies, long-armed, short-legged, and thick-necked. Their teeth were like the fangs of smilodons, curved and saw-edged, extending a finger's length below their massive jaws. (51)

For comparison, consider a scene from Crichton's novel. (To give some context, *Eaters of the Dead* is a re-telling of the Beowulf story as by an Arab adventurer of the Middle Ages living among Vikings.) This scene is set on a foggy night on a flatlands by some hills, when a star-like point appears, is followed by others, and together they form a shape:

> Now Skeld gave a shout, and all the warriors of Buliwylf, myself among them, turned to look at the hills, behind the blanket of mist. Here is what I saw: high in the air, a glowing fiery point of light like a blazing star, and a distance off. All the warriors saw it, and there was a murmuring and exclamation among them.
>   Soon appeared a second point of light, and yet another, and then another. I counted past a dozen and then ceased to count further. These glowing fire-points appeared in a line, which undulated like a snake, or verily like the undulating body of a dragon. (140)

Two paragraphs later, the narrator reports a sound: "The glowing fire-points were still distant, yet they came closer. Now I heard a sound which I took as thunder" (141).
  When Crichton's narrator gets a closer view of one of the horsemen, he notes a non-human detail: "on a black steed rode a human figure in black, but his head was the head of a bear" (141-42). Yet when this rider is struck down, "the bear's head rolled from his body, and I saw that he had beneath the head of a man" (142).

Severian's close look of the monsters in the Saltus mine notes:

> . . . [Their] massive jaws. Yet it was not any of these things, nor the noctilucent light that clung to their fur, that brought the horror I felt. It was something in their faces, perhaps in the huge, pale-irised eyes. It told me they were as human as I . . . these men were wrapped in the guise of lurid apes, and knew it. (51)

Crichton's narrator continues: ". . . head of a bear. I was startled with a time of most horrible fright, and I feared I should die from fear alone, for never had I witnessed such a nightmare vision" (142).

Echo Forward: "Not long ago, when the Samru was still near the mouth of Gyoll" (49) casts forward (IV, chap. 32, 256).

The Walking Tower: This unseen underground monster, whose step causes the man-apes to panic (55), evokes Tolkien's "balrog" and perhaps the Bible's "Behemoth."

Autarch as Master of Things Under the Earth: This has resonance with Jesus having such power "That at the name of Jesus every knee should bow, of things in heaven, and things in earth, and things under the earth" (Philippians 2:10). Note that Severian's narrative has already indicated that the Autarch commands winged females who are conflated with angels: "In the brown book . . . there was the tale of an angel (perhaps actually one of the winged women warriors who are said to serve the Autarch)" (I, chap. 18, 162).

7. The Assassins

Leaving the mine, Severian falls into the ambush set by Agia, who had penned the note from Thecla.

Proust: "Thecla was surely dead" (60). The message from Thecla finds a parallel in *The Fugitive* (1925), where Proust's narrator receives a telegram from his recently deceased girlfriend:

> I opened it as soon as I was in my room, and, glancing through the message which was filled with inaccurately transmitted words, managed nevertheless to make out: "My dear friend, you think me dead, forgive me, I am quite alive, I long to see you, talk about marriage, when do you return? Affectionately. Albertine." (*The Fugitive*, p. 656)

Commentary: When Severian writes, "They say those things [man-apes] come out at night during storms and take animals . . . sometimes . . . children" (63), this trollish detail links to *Eaters of the Dead,* but in this case there is ambiguity enough that perhaps the stolen children, rather than being eaten, are transformed into man-apes. That is, it might be that the man-apes replenish their numbers in a method like those practiced by the torturers and the librarians. Such a system would add additional weight to Severian's observation, "[T]hese men were wrapped in the guise of lurid apes, and knew it" (chap. 6, 51).

8. The Cultellarii

Once back at the inn, Severian slips into a memory daze that is ended when he and Jonas are taken by cutthroats.

Chapter Title: Cultellarii are cutthroats in 12th century (High Middle Ages) France.

Bible: Talking to Jonas, Severian quotes the brown book, "In the beginning was only the hexaemeron" (68). This seems a garbling of Biblical quotes and terms. "In the beginning God created the heaven and the earth" (Genesis 1:1). The term "hexaemeron" is Greek for the six days of creation, which is covered in Genesis 1:1. In the New Testament, the Gospel of John starts, "In the beginning was the Word, and the Word was with God, and the Word was God" (John 1:1).

Regarding the Wall of Nessus: Severian says to Jonas, "When we were going through the Wall, you said the things we saw in there were soldiers, and you implied they had been stationed there to resist Abaia and the others" (69). First of all, this version is at variance with the scene presented earlier (I, chap. 35, 299-300), in which Talos was the one who said the Wall dwellers were soldiers, and nobody mentioned "Abaia and the others." Severian might be trying to provoke a revealing correction, or he might be paradoxing his perfect memory again, but Jonas avoids confirming or denying the statement.

H. G. Wells: Responding to the question above, and others, Jonas says that some leaders, before the autarchs, had engineered warriors "by humanizing animals, and perhaps, in secret by bestializing men" (69), which draws straight from Wells's *The Island of Doctor Moreau* (1896).

Echo: Thecla perfume scent here remembered as "lilies warmed before a fire" (71). Semi-paradoxed, since her scent is usually burning-roses.

Language of Flowers: Lily means "Coquetry" (Day Lily); "Majesty" (Imperial Lily); Purity, Sweetness (White Lily); or Falsehood, Gaiety (Yellow Lily).

9. The Liege of Leaves

Severian and Jonas are taken to meet Vodalus, who gives them the option of joining his rebellion against the Autarch.

Bible: Between the village and the forest they travel through trash hills of the obscene and the dead: "Everything foul lay in tumbled heaps ten times . . . the height of the baluchiter's lofty back" (73). That is, the mounds are 180 feet tall.

[O]bscene statues, canted and crumbling, and human bones to which strips of dry flesh and hanks of hair still clung. And with them ten thousand men and women; those who, in seeking a private resurrection, had rendered their corpses forever imperishable lay here like drunkards after their debauch, their crystal sarcophagi broken, their limbs relaxed in grotesque disarray. (73-74)

This sounds like the tradition of a rubbish heap in Gehenna, the Valley of

Hinnon just south of Jerusalem. For Jesus and his followers, Gehenna was a metaphor for Hell, and this transition of Severian from village to forest throne seems like another "passage through the rings of Hell" sequence, last seen in the Lake of Birds chapters (I, chap. 22-24). Yet the forest is a beautiful, majestic place.

10. Thea

Severian and Jonas join the Vodalarii cause, and their first mission is to deliver a message to a spy in the House Absolute. For their initiation, they must drink the analeptic alzabo and eat the flesh of a dead follower of Vodalus, thereby experiencing the memories of the deceased.

Proust: Severian notes that he first loved Thea because of Vodalus; then loved Thecla because she recalled Thea; now loved Thea again, because she recalled Thecla (81).

Mythology: The Norse Norns (or "Fates") Verthandi (the Present), Skuld (the Future), and Urth (the Past) are names for planets Mars, Venus, and Earth (83).

Bible: Vodalus is afraid of the Claw, saying that people will think him "an enemy of the Theologoumenon" (85). This is a curious phrase.

A "theologoumenon" is a theological statement or concept that lacks absolute doctrinal authority. The Catholic idea of Limbo is an example, once a widespread concept now generally abandoned. So one reading has Vodalus saying that the belief in the Conciliator is a popular yet baseless religion.

Borges: Mention of the alzabo (90) recalls a monster from *The Book of Imaginary Beings,* but it is the Leucrocotta, in the entry "The Crocotta and the Leucrocotta." A fantasy based upon the hyena, Borges quotes the ancient Roman Pliny, "They report that this beast feigneth a mans [sic] voice." It is in T. H. White's *The Bestiary: A Book of Beasts* (1954), being a translation of a medieval bestiary, that we find a note giving a dozen names for this creature, among them "Alzabo."

11. Thecla

The feasting-corpse turns out to be Thecla.

Echo: The taste of the alzabo drink "was as bitter as wormwood . . . recalling a winter day long before when I had been ordered to clean the exterior drain . . . from the journeymen's quarters" (95), which sounds like the day he found Triskele (I, chap. 4, 37).

Bible: The Vodalarii feast is more complex than it might seem at first glance.

There is a communion aspect to it, as remarked by Joan Gordon in 1986 (*Gene Wolfe,* p. 92-93) and Peter Wright in 2003 (*Attending Daedalus,* p. 50). The Vodalarii share a magic drink, they eat the special flesh, they experience a unity. Christian communion arises from the Last Supper, near the end of Jesus' ministry.

There is also a "secret marriage" side to the feast, an event where two bodies become one. For all the other feasters, Thecla was a one-night entertainment; but for Severian, she fused into him. I touch on this briefly in "The Feast of Saint Katharine (with a K)," collected in *Gene Wolfe: 14 Articles*. In part this nuptial notion is building on the context of the water-into-wine thread established in earlier chapters: here is the marriage implied by that scenario, and the ordering of events has been reversed, with the party coming before the marriage. The wedding feast at Cana came early in the ministry of Jesus.

Here is a third angle, that of spiritual baptism. For Christians there is a distinction between water baptism and spirit baptism. Spirit baptism is when the Holy Spirit, third person of the Trinity, takes up residence in the believer. This happened to Jesus at his water baptism by John the Baptist: "And Jesus, when he was baptized, went straightway out of the water: and, lo, the heavens were opened unto him, and he saw the Spirit of God descending like a dove, and lighting on him" (Matthew 3:16). (Note that Thea, half-sister of Thecla, was associated with a dove in the first chapter of the first volume.)

This came before Jesus had begun his ministry, before his Temptation in the Wilderness. For a few years Jesus was the only one with the indwelling Holy Spirit, until the Pentecost, that day when all Christians of that time received the Holy Spirit (Acts 1, 2).

12. The Notules

Travelling again, Severian and Jonas are attacked by notules and are only able to escape by getting the monsters to kill a patrolling soldier.

Chapter Title: Notule is a French word for "little notes," which can be pithy reviews or abstracts.

Commentary: Severian's sacrifice of the uhlan. Always on the lookout for puns, here it is clear he was killed by a few bad reviews.

13. The Claw of the Conciliator

Remorseful, Severian uses the Claw of the Conciliator to resurrect the soldier, then Hethor shows up.

Echo: "Is he dead?" (108) repeats the title of chapter 27 in volume I. The line "I had the sensation of being once more in the Cathedral of the Pelerines" (108) links back to The Destruction of the Altar (I, chap. 18, 166).

Commentary: Shortly after Severian resurrects the uhlan he has his first bout of Thecla invasion.

Proust: Again there is a parallel between Thecla and Proust's Albertine.

Sometimes . . . I felt that the Albertine of long ago, invisible to my eyes, was nevertheless enclosed within me as in the *Piombi* [a prison in the Doge's Palace] of an inner Venice, the tight lid of which some incident occasionally lifted to give me a glimpse of that past.

Thus for instance one evening a letter from my stockbroker reopened for me for an instant the gates of the prison in which Albertine dwelt within me, alive, but so remote, so profoundly buried that she remained inaccessible to me. (*The Fugitive,* p. 654)

14. The Antechamber

Too close to the House Absolute, Severian, Jonas, and Hethor are captured by Praetorian Guards and thrown into the antechamber.

Language of Flowers: Plum blossoms (120) in the gardens of the House Absolute; and a hedge of white roses.

John Bunyan: Severian and Jonas in the antechamber is like Christian and Faithful in the Cage at Vanity Fair in *The Pilgrim's Progress.* Where the pilgrims Christian and Faithful had created a hubbub at the fair and were imprisoned for that, the travelers Severian and Jonas had created a disturbance on the grounds of the House Absolute. Where Bunyan's characters first travel the road together, then arrive at Vanity Fair, before being confined, Wolfe has rearranged the sequence so that they start at Saltus Fair, then travel the road together, before being locked up.

15. Fool's Fire

Talking with the prisoners in the antechamber, Severian realizes that many have been imprisoned for generations, but Jonas becomes very upset, somehow recognizing them through their family histories. A group of demons raid the antechamber, lashing the prisoners with electrified whips.

Bible: Jonas asks if the dimly glowing Claw is dying, to which Severian replies, "No, it's often like this. But when it is active—when it transmuted the water in our carafe and when it awed the man-apes—it shines brightly" (128). Now Severian is stating that the Claw had done the miracle of the wine, and that it had been obvious.

Jonas Discovers His Lost Tribe: The old sailor learns that the prisoners have been in the antechamber for more than seven generations (129). Probing more deeply, he finds the name of the first prisoner was Kim Lee Soong (130). This strikes him a powerful blow, since that name was a common one when he was young (130), back when the Wall of Nessus was built (I, chap. 35, 300). So it seems Jonas has found his lost tribe, and they are living fossils.

L. Frank Baum: The green face in the antechamber (131) is similar to the first appearance of Oz within his famous series of books. In *The Wonderful*

Wizard of Oz (1900), Dorothy enters the green throne room of the Emerald City in order to meet the leader:

> In the center of the chair was an enormous Head, without body to support it or any arms or legs whatever. There was no hair upon this head, but it had eyes and nose and mouth, and was bigger than the head of the biggest giant.
>
> As Dorothy gazed upon this in wonder and fear the eyes turned slowly and looked at her sharply and steadily. Then the mouth moved, and Dorothy heard a terrible voice say:
>
> "I am Oz, the Great and Terrible. Who are you, and why do you seek me?" (chapter 11)

This allusion to Oz perhaps unlocks the Oz-nature of Jonas, his Tin Woodman aspect of being partially living and paradoxically robotic.

16. Jonas

Jonas is wounded and becomes delirious.

Commentary: The blue light of Claw contrast with green light (132).

More About the Lost Tribe: The girl prisoner says to Severian, "When the navigator was buried there were black wagons and people in black clothes walking" (134). This seems to reinforce that the family group descended from a spacefaring man.

Stephan Crane: "Now he [Jonas] slumped against the wall just as I have since seen a corpse sit with its back to a tree" (137). This line is slightly like a signature scene in *The Red Badge of Courage* (1895) where the hero meets a corpse:

> He was being looked at by a dead man who was seated with his back against a columnlike tree. . . . The eyes, staring at the youth, had changed to the dull hue to be seen on the side of dead fish. . . . Over the gray skin of the face ran little ants. (*The Red Badge of Courage,* chap. 7, near end)

We watch for traces of Crane because Wolfe mentioned Crane's novel in talking about *The Book of the New Sun* during a 1986 *Interzone* interview: "You find a similar kind of progression [that of a young man approaching a war] in *The Red Badge of Courage,* but I wanted to develop mine within an sf setting" (Wright's *Shadows of the New Sun,* p. 94).

Lewis Carroll: Jonas referring to the White Knight on the poker (137) is perhaps the most direct allusion to another text, in this case *Through the Looking Glass* (1871), specifically chapter one, where Alice writes, "The white knight is sliding down the poker. He balances very badly."

Jonas on the Dark Ages: Jonas says, "[T]he king was elected at the Marchfield. Counts were appointed by the kings. That was what they called the dark ages. A baron was only a freeman of Lombardy" (137). These are all true. Frankish kings were elected at the Marchfield beginning in the seventh century. Counts were appointed by kings in the Merovingian Dynasty (450-751). The dark ages, also known as the Early Middle Ages, lasted from the fifth century to the tenth century. The word "baron" comes from "baro," Old High German (750-1050) for "freeman," and during that time the Germanic Lombards had their region of Italy.

Jonas says all this after talking about hereditary rulers and hereditary subordinates, so part of his theme is how meritocracy gave way to a hereditary system. It is somewhat paradoxical that the dark ages had the merit-based system and the "more advanced" High Middle Ages introduced a birthright system. Another thread of Jonas's statements seems to be that while the entire Middle Ages lasted a thousand years, the current slump on Urth has lasted much longer.

Echo: "[F]ound me camping on the grass by Ctesiphon's Cross" (139) establishes that the play (I, chap. 32) did in fact occur at Ctesiphon's Cross, just as Talos said it would (I, chap. 16, 149).

Animal Form: Hethor as a hairless rat (139).

Jonas Tells More: Jonas says to Severian, "I have to talk to somebody, so it has to be you even though you'll think I'm a monster when I'm done" (140). Severian responds to this pre-confessional utterance by saying he already knows about the metal parts in his friend. Without confirming or denying that this is what makes him monstrous, Jonas says, "We crashed. It had been so long, on Urth, that there was no port when we returned, no dock" (140).

This requires some unpacking. It implies vast historical change. If my readings are correct, when Jonas left Urth, Citadel Hill was the port of Urth, the city was not called Nessus, and the Wall had recently been built. When Jonas returned to Urth, Citadel Hill had "towers" that were once ships and there was no place to land, so they crash landed. Yet there is still interstellar visitation during the time of the autarchs, which suggests a different type of ships. Putting this together, there are strong indications that Jonas left in the "rocket" time of history and returned in the "sail" time of posthistory.

Jonas goes on to admit that, contrary to Severian's expectations, he was a robot that was repaired with biological parts. Then, speaking of Jolenta, he says, "I have never loved before, never in all the time since our crew scattered" (140).

Combining many elements together, Kim Lee Soong was a member of his rocket crew on the *Fortunate Cloud;* after the crash, the crew scattered; Kim Lee Soong ended up in the antechamber; when the navigator Kim Lee Soong died there was pomp and ceremony; Jonas has been wandering the

Commonwealth for over 140 years.

17. The Tale of the Student and His Son

To pass the time, Severian reads aloud to Jonas a story from the brown book.

In the redoubt of the magicians, the Student is pressured to produce a dream son or leave. Putting aside his procrastination, the Student fleshes a hero who sets forth to remove the curse on his city. This Son takes command of a ship and sails to the island where he meets the princess, daughter of the monster, and she gives him valuable clues. He searches through the maze, then engages the ogre in mighty battle. Victorious, he returns to his city, but the Student kills himself after misinterpreting the darkened sails as meaning that the Son had died.

Literary Pun: The student and his thesis.

Jack Vance: "Turjan of Miir" in *The Dying Earth* begins with hero Turjan facing his latest failure at creating a synthetic man. His desire to improve his technique propels him forward to find a better spell from the powerful sorcerer Pandelume.

Borges: "The Circular Ruins" (1940) has a nameless sorcerer who works at crafting a son from dreamstuff.

Myth: Theseus and the Minotaur (a hero versus the monster in the maze) from ancient Greece. This source provides the basic structure of the tale.

Americana: The *Monitor* and the *Merrimack* (a sea battle between ironclads in the American Civil War) at the Battle of Hampton Roads (1862). The *Merrimack* was a Union ship captured by the Confederacy and renamed "Virginia," equating to the *Land of Virgins* in the tale. The Union's *Monitor* had a single turret on the middle of the deck, very much like the naviscaput's tower. Their battle ended indecisively.

High Contrast: The detail about "A book he had not unshelved in decades" (145) makes us wonder at the advanced age of this student. Apparently he had dawdled for decades.

Greek: "A diffident helot" (145). This is a Greek term, but it is specific to Sparta. Another Greek word, "Hesperus" (151), is an ancient astronomical name for Venus as an "evening star" (rather than as a morning star).

Norse: "On the whale road" (147) is a phrase associated with *Beowulf*.

Wolf: Dire wolves (151); wolves howl (153).

18. Mirrors

By sifting Thecla's memories, Severian learns that the demons were just mischievous young exultants having their cruel fun. He finds the secret door leading out of the antechamber, but in the next room they come to, the Presence Chamber, Jonas sees his opportunity to escape Urth and enters the mirror teleportation device.

Greek: Jonas mentions Athens as the home of the hero (160), but this highlights the odd Spartan detail of "helot," perhaps conflating Athens and Sparta with their Peloponnesian War with the American North and South with their Civil War.

Echo: Jonas's disappointment with Severian (160) repeats the green man's disappointment with Severian (II, chap. 3).

Dubious Saint: When the girl says, "Please, where did the lady go?" (165), this seems like a good time to tell more about "The Acts of Paul and Thecla." While one version of the legend has Thecla swallowed by the mountain, "Another account said that a secret passage led back to Rome, where she was buried close to St. Paul" (*Oxford Dictionary of Saints, Third Edition*). The point here being that the woman is united in death with the man who brought her to faith, which seems surprisingly like the situation with Wolfe's Thecla and Severian.

Echo Forward: Meet again with Nicarete (165), a cast ahead into the frame tale.

Enamel: The enameled twisted signs on the panel (167) probably say "Urth."

Myth: While magic mirrors were talked about much earlier, the direct experience of this chapter seems to complete the "Three Sacred Treasures of Japan" pattern (sword, mirror, jewel) mentioned in notes for volume I, chapter 31.

Algis Budrys: Jonas presents ties to the Budrys novels *Who?* (1958) and *Rogue Moon* (1960).

From "Algis Budrys I" in *Castle of Days,* Gene Wolfe writes:

> *Who?* (1958) is the book that made him famous, at least within the SF community. It is perhaps as fine a study of dehumanization and alienation as science fiction will ever produce. A brilliant American scientist is torn by a laboratory explosion and repaired with what we would now call "bionic" parts by the Soviets. He is returned to the U.S.—but the U.S. cannot be sure of that; so much of him is gone that what remains cannot be identified.
>
> All this is simple enough, if you like. It is even—if you like—a retelling of L. Frank Baum's story of the Tin Woodman, who when he had sliced his "meat" humanity completely away could no longer recall his true name (which was Nick Chopper). The difference lies in intent, and the treatments that result from it. (325)

Wolfe makes the strong connection between the Budrys novel *Who?* and the Tin Woodman of Oz, both of which clearly relate to the character Jonas. But wait, there is more: in the same article, Wolfe goes on to talk about another Budrys novel that seems relevant to Jonas: *Rogue Moon* (1960).

In *Rogue Moon,* a "matter transmitter" has been invented in a near future in which rocketry is still primitive; and an unmanned probe has managed to drop a transmitting and receiving station on the far side of the moon. The first explorers to go through the transmitter discover an alien construct millions of years old, a thing compounded of building, machine, and hallucination. It soon kills everyone who ventures inside. (326)

So in addition to a Budrys novel about ambiguous cyborgs, Wolfe mentions a Budrys novel about deadly teleportation.

If all that seems tenuous, please note that Budrys's middle name was "Jonas."

John Bunyan: When Jonas goes from prison to disintegration it echoes the fate of pilgrim Faithful, who is taken from the Cage and burned at the Stake. Pilgrim Christian knows his friend has gone ahead to the higher world of the Celestial City.

But now, having established some correlation between Jonas and Faithful, I look back through *The Pilgrim's Progress,* searching for other traces. I find that Faithful's first adventure was at the Wicket Gate, where he met Wanton, who offered him "all carnal and fleshy" pleasures. In hindsight, this appears similar yet opposite to when Jonas met Jolenta at the Gate of Nessus (I, chap. 35, 300), which he later confessed as love-at-first-sight: "I have never loved before [seeing her at the Gate], never in all the time since our crew scattered" (II, chap. 16, 140).

19. Closets

Severian wanders alone through the subterranean House Absolute, encountering Odilo and finding *Terminus Est.*

Echo: Encountering khaibit Thea on the stairs (170) mirrors a similar action in the Echopraxia (I, chap. 9).

Wolf: White wolves of the Second House (175).

20. Pictures

Rudesind the curator again gives Severian directions, and Severian meets up with the brothel manager from the Algedonic Quarter, learning that he is the spy Vodalus wanted him to contact.

Echo: Encountering Rudesind (178) repeats the action at their first meeting in the citadel (I, chap. 5).

Thematic Echo: Rudesind looking for his own portrait (179) is similar to the unnamed boatman searching for his wife Cas in the Lake of Birds (I, chap. 22, 196-200).

Echo: Encountering the pimp (181) recalls the action of their first meeting at the echopraxia brothel (I, chap. 9).

Non-Byzantine: The term "androgyne" (183) shows a detail of difference between the Commonwealth and Byzantium. That is, eunuchs were a feature of Byzantine society, but the Romans were repulsed by this.

21. Hydromancy

Through an accidental miscommunication, the spy opens *The Book of Mirrors* for Severian, but Severian balks at entering it, instead choosing to remain on Urth. Severian realizes that this "spy" is actually the Autarch himself.

Animal Form: The "pavonine dyings" (187) to the cover of *The Book of Mirrors* links to peacocks, last seen with Agia's brocade gown (I, chap. 16, 152).

Bible: The blood on Severian's forehead (188), correctly termed "haematidrosis" and "blood sweat," is associated with Jesus at the garden of Gethsemane, just before his arrest by Roman soldiers: "And being in agony he prayed more earnestly: and his sweat was as it were great drops of blood falling down to the ground" (Luke 22:44). Note the parallel of "garden" here: Severian is asking for directions to "the garden."

Rose: A water sign in the Vatic Fountain (191).

Stage-manager (Autarch): The ruler of the Commonwealth (190) is also a brothel owner in the slums of Nessus and a spy for Vodalus at the House Absolute.

Language of Flowers: Lilies (192).

22. Personifications

Severian finds Doctor Talos's troupe. He sits with Dorcas in a garden of herbs.

Animals: The megather roars (193).

Language of Flowers: Dorcas wears domesticated plum blossoms, which means "keep your promise." The herb garden has plants offering positive notes, like rosemary ("remembrance"), angelica ("inspiration"), mint ("virtue"), as well as negative notes, with basil ("hatred") and rue ("disdain").

Commentary: Dorcas shares her dreams (197-98).

23. Jolenta

Severian has a tryst with the actress Jolenta on a boat in a river.

Animals: White deer in garden of House Absolute (203).

George Orwell: A grove of chestnuts (205). Orwell's potent symbol for the betrayal of lovers: "under the spreading chestnut tree, I sold you and you sold me" (*Nineteen Eighty-Four,* Part 1, chapter 7).

Hawthorn Hedge: Thomas Rhymer and Fairy Queen?

Contrarian Severian: Severian going off to tryst with Jolenta is ironic since Talos had just said, "Do you know what I like about you, Sieur Severian? You prefer Dorcas [over Jolenta]" (II, chap. 22, 195).

Hieronymous Bosch: The river idyll, with lines like "couples lay on the soft grass" (208), reminds me of the central panel of *The Garden of Earthly Delights* (circa 1500) by Hieronymus Bosch. The river might even run in a circle.

A brief description by Thomas Köster regarding this famous artwork:

Hieronymous Bosch created three different ideas of the world in his *Garden of Earthly Delights*. On the left-hand panel he painted paradise, with God bringing Adam and Eve together in the foreground. The gigantic central section is simply teeming with naked people and exotic animals.

The right-hand wooden panel shows hell, where people have turned to vice, houses burn and wars rage. (Köster, *50 Artists You Should Know*, 2006)

24. Dr. Talos's Play

Severian takes his parts in the play, the script of which is given.

Bible: Nephilim (212), the offspring of the "sons of God" and the "daughters of men" (Genesis 6:1-4) before the Deluge. They are usually described as giants.

"East of Paradise" (223) alludes to the Land of Nod, east of Eden (Genesis 4: 16). Later in the play the term "the land of Nod" (233) shows up.

Myth: Meschia, Meschiane, and Jahi all come straight from the Persian creation myth of Zoroaster. In short, the good god Ahura Mazda created the world and the primordial being called Gayomart. Jahi, a she-demon of lust, poisoned Gayomart for her master, the evil god Ahriman. From the corpse of Gayomart grew a tree; from this tree grew Meschia and Meschiane, father and mother of humans.

Greek: Demiurge (a Universal Fashioner), Paraclete (an advocate or helper), Fiend (an evil spirit), and Erinys (the Furies, female chthonic deities of vengeance).

Commentary: It is daring to include a playscript within a novel. James Joyce did it in *Ulysses* (1922), and Thomas Pynchon did it in *The Crying of Lot 49* (1966).

In Wolfe's case "Eschatology and Genesis" is remarkable for being a text that magically shapes and reflects Severian's life, even more so than the tales of the brown book. Like the play at the Feast of Holy Katharine, it serves as an instruction through repetition for the actors.

To bring it all together into summary conclusion, the drama is a vaudeville mystery play, a jumble of Hebrew Old Testament and Persian Zoroastrian elements, with a few Greek bits as garnish. The title "Eschatology and Genesis" implies that it will begin with judgment and then move forward to a new creation, but there is a reversal, where the opening scene is a vaudeville skit about Eden.

25. The Attack of the Hierodules

The play ends prematurely in a firefight with aliens in the audience.

Thematic Echo: With "he swung it like a mace" (239) Baldanders mimics Agilus attacking the crowd (I, chap. 27, 240).

Hieronymous Bosch: The details about "a circular mouth rimmed with needle teeth; eyes that were themselves a thousand eyes . . .; jaws like tongs" (239) bring to my mind's eye the third panel of *The Garden of Earthly Delights*, the one with the hellish night scene.

Dreams: Afterwards, Severian dreams of fighting Baldanders on a castle by a lake (243).

26. Parting

The troupe breaks up the next day, with Talos and Baldanders heading for Lake Diuturna, and Severian, Dorcas, and Jolenta walking toward Thrax.

Stage-manager (Autarch): Jolenta says she met "a high official of the sort that cares nothing for women" (245), probably the Autarch she was so eager to meet even if he were unmanned (chap. 23, 206). Talos talks of having met an agamite (247), again probably the Autarch.

Untraced Allusion: Talos claims to quote a poet: "Now we have come to the place where men are pulled apart by their destinations" (248). I can find no source to this line.

Bible: Dorcas talks of the Conciliator, saying among other things that he might be encountered as an animal, speaking the human tongue, and he appeared to some pious woman or other in the form of roses (253).

The first might be a garbling of Jesus as the Lamb of God. The second seems related to the miracle of roses associated with saints Elizabeth of Hungary (1207-1231) and Elizabeth of Portugal (1271-1336).

The brown book contains a section mentioning the Conciliator, but Severian puts it aside to read later (253).

27. Toward Thrax

That night, Severian is awakened by the undine calling him from the river.

Memories: Severian's thinking on Holy Katharine's day leads to a previously undiscovered memory of nursing at his mother's breast (257). This might suggest a connection between his mother and Holy Katharine.

28. The Odalisque of Abaia

The undine tempts Severian, offering him the ability to breathe water, but he is reluctant. She unsuccessfully tries to seize him before swimming away. Meanwhile, Jolenta has attempted suicide.

Francis Bacon: The brown book has the line, "These times are the ancient times, when the world is ancient." This is a portion of a quote from Francis Bacon: "These times are the ancient times, when the world is ancient, and not those which we account ancient *ordine retrogrado,* by a computation backwards from ourselves," (Bacon, *Advancement of Learning,* Book I, 1605).

Christopher Marlowe: The brown book gives the sentence "Hell has no limits, nor is circumscribed; for where we are is Hell, and where Hell is, there we must be" (II, chap. 28, 266). This is line 553 of Christopher Marlowe's *Doctor Faustus* (1592).

Dreams: Dorcas tells of her dream wherein her baby was too young for dolls (266).

29. The Herdsmen

The group stays in a peasant's sod house, where the Claw performs a few minor miracles.

Commentary: Jolenta seems a different person when Severian sees her from the corner of his eye (269). Previously this effect was reported by the little girl in the antechamber when Thecla possessed Severian (chap. 18, 165). The implication is that Jolenta is "possessed" through non-magical means (hypnotism). Compare with Thecla and the Revolutionary, an electro-shock type of device that induces suicidal behavior by "awakening" an indwelling persona.

Animals: Severian decapitates a charging bull (270).

30. The Badger Again

The group enters the stone town and encounters the Cumaean, her assistant Merryn the witch, and Hildegrin.

Commentary: Jolenta "seeks her lover" (283) in Talos.

31. The Cleansing

Dorcas gives Hildegrin a secret message from the spy at the House Absolute. Hildegrin boasts that he had followed them to the Sanguinary Field, helped the capture of Agilus, watched the execution, saw the play at Ctesiphon's Cross, and did not lose them until the trouble at the Piteous Gate.

The six of them together participate in a group ritual summoning of Apu-Punchau, an avatar from the past, but when he appears, Hildegrin attacks him and Severian finds himself wrestling with Hildegrin. A crack of thunder brings him back to the stone town, where he finds himself alone with Dorcas—Hildegrin is destroyed, the Cumaean and Merryn have fled, and Jolenta has finally died.

Stage-manager (Autarch): The Autarch also met with Dorcas (285).

Stage-manager (Hildegrin): Hildegrin brags about how much he has done (286), yet he is on the other team.

Hildegrin talks of being short-handed, "what with my two fellows bein' killed on the road" (287). Curious detail. Might we know them? Probably not the assassins at the Saltus mine, those men hired by Agia. Probably not Hethor and Beuzec, with the emphasis on "killed" rather than a more ambiguous "lost."

Brown Book: Reference to *Empires of Foliage and Flower* (289), a tale of the brown book which is not included in Severian's narrative.

Mythology: Abraxas (289) is a Gnostic god associated with Mithra and Jehovah.

Thematic Echo: When Severian sees the metal parts ("wires and bands of metal") in Jolenta (291), it is like what he saw ("something of wires and flashing") when Jonas dematerialized at the end of chapter 18.

Bible: In the ruins Severian sees dust that rises up to form insects, tumbling in large clumps on the ground, but then it changes: "The swarms that had seethed with life a moment before now showed bleached ribs; the dust motes . . . formed skulls that gleamed green in the moonlight . . . . One by one they rose" (292).

This powerful sequence seems to derive from the Book of Ezekiel:

> The hand of the Lord was upon me, and carried me out in the spirit of the Lord, and set me down in the midst of the valley which was full of bones,
>
> And caused me to pass by them round about: and, behold, there were very many in the open valley; and, lo, they were very dry.
>
> And he said unto me, Son of man, can these bones live? And I answered, O Lord God, thou knowest.
>
> Again he said unto me, Prophesy upon these bones, and say unto them, O ye dry bones, hear the word of the Lord.
>
> Thus saith the Lord God unto these bones; Behold, I will cause breath to enter into you, and ye shall live:
>
> And I will lay sinews upon you, and will bring up flesh upon you, and cover you with skin, and put breath in you, and ye shall live; and ye shall know that I am the Lord. (Ezekiel 37:1-6)

Jack Vance: The rebuilding of the stone town in this chapter is like a sequence from "Ulan Dhor" in *The Dying Earth*. This tale features a ruinous city torn by many millennia of civil war, and the city's immortal founder, awakened by the hero Ulan Dhor, begins to refurbish the place through techno-magical means:

> "Five thousand years and the wretches still quarrel? Time has taught them no wisdom! Then stronger agencies must be used . . . Behold!". . . . The tentacles sprouted a thousand appendages . . . These ranged the city, and wherever there was crumbling or mark of age the tentacles dug, tore, blasted, burnt; then spewed new materials into place. (Vance, *The Dying Earth,* p. 104)

The difference is that Wolfe eschews the technological for the supernatural. By continuing in the mode of Ezekiel, the result is more like Clark Ashton Smith than Jack Vance.

Clark Ashton Smith: Half of the Zothique stories involve necromancy, but it is "The Empire of the Necromancers" (1932) that uses imagery straight from Ezekiel 37.

Rose: An odor as of myrrh and roses (293).

Echo: Apu-Punchau (293) has the face depicted on that funeral bronze.

Incest or Paradox: Severian refers back to the jungle hut in the Botanic Gardens, writing of "the woman and her brother" (294). This implies that Marie and Robert, previously identified as wife and husband, are involved in brother/sister incest, or it is another case of perfect memory paradox. Spotted by Roy C. Lackey at the Urth List (12 MAR 1999).

Little Red Riding Hood: The scarlet tassels (295).

Appendixes: "Social Relationships in the Commonwealth" and "Money, Measures, and Time."

Wolfe gives glosses on the exultants, the armigers, the optimates, the commonality, the servants of the throne, the religious, and the cacogens. He numismatically notes chrisos, asimi, orichalks, and aes. Taking the long view, he defines league, span, chain, ell, pace, stride, cubit; chiliad, age, month, week, and watch.

VOLUME III: THE SWORD OF THE LICTOR

Into the distance disappear the mounds of human heads.
I dwindle–go unnoticed now.
But in affectionate books, in children's games,
I will rise from the dead to say: the sun!
[sic] Osip Mandelstam

Epigraph: A quote from Osip Mandelstam, as cited in the text. Mandelstam (1891-1938) was a Russian poet who died in a gulag, alluded to in Wolfe's *Castle of Days* (229-30). The quoted text is the complete poem, referenced as "(341) 1937" in the "posthumous poems" section of *Selected Poems* by Osip Mandelshtam [sic], Penguin, 1991.

1. Master of the House of Chains

A few months after the incident at the stone town, Severian and Dorcas are getting settled into life at Thrax, but their relationship is being strained by both his profession and her unknown past which she is slowly remembering.

Language of Flowers: There is a metaphorical flower image around Dorcas, as Severian sees the city of Thrax as petals of a jonquil (7), meaning "I desire a return of affection." Severian notes, "[S]he did not seem to see them."

Religious Buildings: Thrax has a pantheon (9), which is probably a temple dedicated to all the gods like the one in ancient Rome (following the Roman thread of Commonwealth culture); a partial list of all the gods in the Commonwealth would include Abraxas, Adonai, Apeiron, Caitanya, Demiurge, Gea, Hypogeon, Increate, Jurupari, Oannes, Paraclete, Theoanthropos, and Ylem.

Prisons: The contrast of the Vincula with the antechamber and the

Matachin Tower (12) reinforces the recurring trope of prisons in the text.

Commentary: This chapter is surprisingly non-linear. It begins with Dorcas talking about her shower, but we do not know what her line "It was in my hair" refers to until the end of the chapter.

2. Upon the Cataract

After a long walk through Thrax, Severian finds Dorcas despondent by the waterside.

Language of Flowers: Dorcas wears a peony (16), meaning "Shame, Anger."

Echo: Memory (20) links to Palaemon's talk of Thrax being at the shore, then the mountains (I, chap. 13, 124). The view from the top of the donjon like that from the top of the Matachin Tower (21) links back to his last look before exile (I, chap. 13, 126-27).

3. Outside the Jacal

Severian arranges for Dorcas to stay at the Duck's Nest inn. Trying to find his way back to the Vincula, he meets a poor boy named Jader who has a deathly ill sister.

The Other Shoe Drops: Morwenna poisoned her child (27).

Paradoxes to Perfect Memory: Severian writes, "I remembered the uhlan . . . dead until I touched his lips with the Claw" (III, chap. 3, 32). But it was upon the uhlan's forehead, not his lips (II, chap. 13, 111). Severian continues, "I had not used it or even considered using it since it had failed to save Jolenta," and this seems a paradox, since Severian had successfully used the Claw on the herdsman (II, chap. 29) after he had applied it to Jolenta (II, chap. 28, 263), but maybe Severian is considering Jolenta's death (II, chap. 31) as the point of the Claw's failure.

4. In the Bartizan of the Vincula

Back at the Vincula, the archon of Thrax invites Severian to attend a costume party at the palace, and there perform a quiet execution without using any tools.

Poem: Dorcas leaves poetry lines in soap on the mirror, "Lift me to the fallen wood" (34).

Rose: Rosolio (38) is a type of Italian liqueur derived from rose petals.

Echo: Image of mask on pass (37) the same as the face of a hierodule at the attack (II, chap. 25); the water stairs (40) linked to Gyoll steps (I, chap. 2).

5. Cyriaca

At the costume party, Severian meets Cyriaca, an armigette in the uniform of a Pelerine.

Jack Vance: A masquerade features in the Dying Earth story "Turjan of Miir," when Turjan is sent by the sorcerer Pandelume to steal a magical amulet:

> It was night in white-walled Kaiin, and festival time. Orange lanterns floated in the air, moving as the breeze took them . . . The streets surged with the wine-flushed populace, costumed in a multitude of bizarre modes. Here was a Melantine bargeman, here a warrior of Valdaran's Green Legion, here another of ancient times wearing one of the old helmets . . . a garlanded courtesan of the Kauchique littoral danced the Dance of the Fourteen Silken Movements . . . In the shadow of a balcony a girl barbarian embraced a man blackened and in leather harness as a Deodand of the forest. (12)

Vance works an exotic scene of Arabian Nights-infused hedonism. Compare this with the following passage from Wolfe:

> I saw men and women costumed as autochthons, with their faces stained russet and dabbed with white, and even one man who was an autochthon and yet was dressed like one, in a costume no more and no less authentic than the others . . . . officers dressed as women and women dressed as soldiers, eclectics . . . , gymnosophists, ablegates and their acolytes, eremites, eidolons, zoanthrops half beast and half human, and deodands and remontados in picturesque rags. (42)

See how Wolfe name-drops "deodands" in open homage to Vance.

For another curious congruence, note that Vance's Turjan is at the festival in order to steal an amulet; whereas Wolfe's Severian wears a hidden amulet:

> Then, while I was grinning to myself behind my mask, it seemed that the Claw, in its soft leathern sack, drove against my breastbone to remind me that the Conciliator had been no jest, and that I bore some fragment of his power with me. (42)

Thematic Echo: "[R]aise the celure over the garden" (46) whispers of the Pelerine tent.

Language of Wine: Sangaree (44) is a historical precursor to sangria.

6. The Library of the Citadel

Severian hears Cyriaca's tale and has an amorous adventure with her.

Background Characters: We see a sanbenito and a midinette (49) pass by. Since the sanbenito is a heretic named after the coat he wears, and a midinette can be a seamstress, we have the odd sight of a coat and a coat-maker.

Language of Wine: Cuvee (50), a blend or batch. "Estate cuvee" sounds like a high quality, a "reserve wine." Later they share an unnamed wine "almost clear as water" (53), so stimulating that "to drink it was like drinking strength from the heart of a bull" (53).

Bible: The gathered writings in Cyriaca's story were "eisegesistic" (54). Eisegesis is "reading into" the text; the process of interpreting a text in a way that includes one's own presuppositions, agendas, or biases into the text. This is in contrast with "exegesis," drawing out meaning from a text.

Echo: Cyriaca's story links back to the Library (I, chap. 6).

Arabian Nights: Cyriaca plays Scheherazade in her talking and seduction. Cyriaca does not grasp it, but Severian is from the land of her fable.

7. Attractions

Severian learns Cyriaca is the one he must execute.

Adultery: Cyriaca links her adultery to her husband's halting her visit to the Well of Orchids (59). It is her revenge. This indicates her vanity has spurred her to infidelity.

Echo: Severian tells Cyriaca about the stone town (59-61), a link to the ruins (II, chap. 31). She gives her interpretation, that Severian was the "witch" and the sick woman his client, and the other woman his servant (61-62).

8. Upon the Cliff

Leaving the palace, Severian goes to Jader's hut and uses the Claw on his sister, miraculously healing her.

Bible: Jesus healed two youngsters. The daughter of Jairus was twelve years old (Mark 5:21-43), and the son of the widow from Nain was a young man (Luke 7:11-17).

Commentary: The narrative has skipped ahead. When Severian notes "[A thought] lifted some part of the depression I would otherwise have felt" (64), it implies he executed Cyriaca and is looking for distraction; but "It seemed likely that by this time they were searching for me" (65) suggests something else. There is a hint that Severian's healing of the children atones for what he did to Cyriaca. In a way this is like the beginning of volume I, which starts at the gate in chapter 1, then backtracks to Gyoll in chapter 2.

9. The Salamander

Severian tries to make his way to the Duck's Nest inn, but he encounters a fiery monster that has been searching for him. The creature follows him into a cliff house, where its own heat burns out the floor, causing the salamander to fall down the cliff to its death.

Echo: "I had seen a pistol fired" (69) links to that night at the necropolis (I, chap. 1); "[I]t had waked whatever slept beneath the mine" (71) links to the Saltus Mine (II, chap. 6).

Flower: The salamander "seemed to open as a flower might" (71).

Burning Rose: The "heat flower" imagery is close to "burning rose."

Enamel: "[T]hose many-colored serpents we see brought from the jungles . . . seem works of colored enamel" (71-72).

10. Lead

At the Duck's Nest inn, Dorcas tells Severian she has vomited a lead slug.

Flaubert: Dorcas reports that the sling-stones were "stamped with the word *strike*" (78). This tidbit also shows up in Flaubert's historical novel *Salammbo* (1862), regarding ancient Carthage under siege:

> The most annoying were the bullets of the slingers . . . . These cruel projectiles bore engraved letters which stamped themselves on the flesh;—and insults might be read on corpses such as "pig," "vermin," and sometimes jests: "Catch it!" (Chap. 13: Moloch)

11. The Hand of the Past

Dorcas admits her terrible secret—she was one of the dead in the Garden of Endless Sleep, a corpse accidentally brought to life by the Claw. She must seek her past back in Nessus, and Severian must flee to the north for allowing Cyriaca to escape.

Paradox: "You think the Claw brought you back" (83). Paradoxed because Dorcas was out of the water first.

Jack Vance: With this new information, we reevaluate the chapter "Dorcas" (I, chap. 22). The detail of an old man (the boatman) searching a shore for decades, met by a newly arrived adventurer (Severian) who finds the treasure without trying, recalls a bit from the adventures of Vance's rogue Cugel.

In *The Eyes of the Overworld* (1966), in the section named "Cil," Cugel arrives at a beach where a solitary old man sifts sand, clearly searching for something. The beachcomber tells Cugel of his quest to find an amulet lost by his great-great-grandfather. The search has been carried out across the generations. The man tells Cugel of the local geography, and how the area was the domain of Cil, owned by his ancestor. Cugel, idly kicking at the sand, discovers the amulet. The man begs him for it, but Cugel refuses to hand it over, and continues on his way.

At the end of the section, Cugel leaves the domain of Cil with a beautiful woman he had endured adversarial relations with in the previous section.

Vance's Cugel has an artifact that belongs to others, and he is trying to learn how to use it, but by the end of the section he has returned it and escaped with the woman, cast out. Severian's situation follows this: in "Dorcas," Severian has a relic (but does not know it), and he is travelling with a woman (Agia) who is adversarial toward him (but he does not know it).

T. S. Eliot: Recalling that Dorcas drew a hyacinth from the water (I, chap. 24), in Eliot's poem "The Waste Land" (1922), hyacinth means "resurrection." While this is contrary to the Language of Flowers, it certainly has bearing here. Noticed by Roy C. Lackey.

Bible: Biblical Dorcas is found in Acts 9:36-42. A widow known for her sewing, she was resurrected by Saint Peter.

Death and Innocence Trade Sides: The conversation between Severian and Dorcas picks up threads started in previous volumes, beginning with Dr. Talos referring to them as Death and Innocence (I, chap. 32, 274). Dorcas chafed under these labels.

They next spoke on this at the orchard on the grounds of the House Absolute. Dorcas said, "But you're not really Death. . . . To me you're Life" (II, chap. 22, 200). After Severian suggested it was a metaphor, she argued, "But it was a dangerous, *bad* metaphor, and it was aimed at you like a lie" (201). After this conversation, Severian wondered about her unexpressed thoughts on the "Innocence" tag, and we suspect that she found "Innocence" awkward for herself when she had admitted to Severian that she was not a virgin (I, chap. 30, 259), and this after Agia's calling her a virgin at the Inn of Lost Loves (I, chap. 25, 222).

But at their last conversation, Severian says, "There was a time when you told me I was not death" (III, chap. 11, 85), and she tells him that he has become Death to her. Then again, she implies she is Death now, that she is a corpse cruelly restored to life. Are they both Death, then?

No. Severian is Innocence, because Innocence is more than just virginity.

12. Following the Flood

Severian tells what Cyriaca had told him, that the Autarch serves the cacogens, even as the cacogens aid the Autarch's enemies, the Ascians. Dorcas and Severian go their separate ways, she by boat and he by the prison sewage drain of the Vincula itself.

Echo: Contrast of leaving Thrax (95) with when Severian first left the citadel on his day of exile (I, chap. 14, 130).

Bible: Severian shows mercy toward Cyriaca, similar to how Jesus spares the adulteress in John 8:3-11. The "flood" of the title alludes to Noah's Flood; the actual water release washing the prisoners evokes a mass-baptism.

Commentary: This chapter forms the "escape from jail and city on alert" scenario. Severian's deal with Cyriaca means that she is going into his past (living in Nessus) and he is going into her past (following the Pelerines); they are trading places.

13. Into the Mountains

Alone in the mountains, Severian feels Hethor magically tracking him.

Myth: Severian writes about the flora along "the south bank of the Cephissus" (91). In Greece there are two rivers so named, but in Ovid's *Metamorphoses* this "river of gardens" is an important location at the end of Deucalion's Flood. After the waters receded, the last humans, Deucalion and Pyrrha, prayed at the shrine of Themis beside the Cephissus. At Themis's instruction they threw stones over their shoulders, and these became the men and women of the new human race.

Tarot: The moment Severian nearly steps off the cliff (104) re-enacts the image of the tarot card The Fool. Wolfe is familiar enough with the Tarot to have written an award-winning poem on the subject, "The Computer Iterates the Greater Trumps" (1978).

Leagues, Non-Literal: Severian writes about the cliff, "[H]ere half a mountain had dropped away . . . falling a league at least" (105). A league is three miles, so this vertical distance would be three times the depth of the Grand Canyon. While this might be barely plausible, it shifts to the implausible when we add the detail of Lune's orbit being "fifty thousand leagues away" (III, chap. 32, 253), where the orbital period suggests it is more like eighty thousand leagues, as it is for our Moon today. These are cases where it seems the leagues are figurative rather than literal. It may be hard to believe this when Severian's culture has such Copernican exactitude as to eschew such terms as "sunrise" and "sunset" for such beautiful lines as surpass the phrases of Arabian Nights, for example, "the west was lifted to cover the sun" (I, chap. 14, 130); "it was very early still, the old sun had hardly dropped Urth's veil from his face" (II, chap. 1, 8); "[t]he western horizon had already climbed more than half up the sky" (II, chap. 4, 30); and "Urth's laboring margin has climbed once more above the red disc" (II, chap. 23, 209). Yet it seems to be the case that Severian can use "leagues" in a non-literal sense.

David Lindsay: This begins a sequence of chapters similar in some strange way to chapters 9 through 19 of Lindsay's *A Voyage to Arcturus* (1920). Wolfe recommends this novel in a 1973 interview (Wright's *Shadows of the New Sun*, 17) and speaks of it in a 1992 interview (ibid, 104).

14. The Widow's House

After descending a perilous cliff, he finds the house and family of pioneer Becan (wife Casdoe, son little Severian, daughter Severa, and Casdoe's father) and receives shelter.

15. He is Ahead of You!

At the cabin it turns out that Agia is hiding upstairs, and as she begins to attack Severian, an alzabo cries at the door in the voice of Severa.

Paradoxes to Perfect Memory: When Severian is expounding to Agia his theory on Hethor avoiding Jonas, he says Hethor "made no attempt to sit with us" in the antechamber (120). But earlier, Severian wrote of Hethor and Jonas together in the antechamber, when Hethor "came to join us" (II, chap. 18, 161). He might be overstating the case to Agia in order to get a reaction out of her.

16. The Alzabo

Using the voice of Becan, the alzabo gets into the house. The others leave Severian downstairs like a sacrifice for it, but he makes a deal with the monster: that he will leave the house in the morning and will not hunt it in the future.

Little Red Riding Hood: The alzabo as the magical wolf, hoping to eat the whole family.

Jack Vance: The showdown between hero and monster is something like that between hero and Deodand in the story "Mazirian the Magician" of *The Dying Earth*.

17. The Sword of the Lictor

The next day Casdoe, her father, and her son abandon their home. Severian follows far behind. The family is set upon by nine zoanthrops, but as Severian runs to help them, the alzabo charges into the fray, defending the family. Severian and little Severian are the only survivors. Severian adopts the orphan.

Wolf: I believe it was Neil Gaiman on the GEnie BBS who pointed out in the 1990s that the alzabo in this episode is a "gene-hunting" wolf. This is a great example of Gaiman's "find the author" strategy.

Commentary: The Casdoe episode of four chapters strikes me as being akin to *A Voyage to Arcturus* because of the transformations Severian is put through: he is suddenly given a family, he faces a demonic Agia (who seems more like Jahi than before), and then he loses most of his new family to a nightmarish monster that blends Arabian Nights with "Little Red Riding

Hood." This is the chapter that names the volume, and it is very grim.

18. Severian and Severian

Severian and his adopted son hike up the mountain.

Wolf: Wolves (145), constellations Wolf and Little Wolf (146), Severian and son as Wolf and Little Wolf (146).

Cross: The constellation (146).

Apollo: Little Severian says of his sister Severa, "We were twins" (146). On the surface this suggests that in the Commonwealth the names Severian and Severa are known as twin names, perhaps as common as Agilus and Agia. It also implies that Severian was born a twin. Curiously enough, Apollo, the god of the Sun and of wolves, was also a twin, his sister being Artemis, goddess of the Moon.

19. The Tale of the Boy Called Frog

Severian reads his adoptive son a story from the brown book.

"Early Summer," a queen beyond Urth, had a child by a flower. She named him "Spring Wind." He in turn impregnated an Urth princess "Bird of the Wood" with twins that she put into a basket in the river. The twins were found by two poor sisters who took them in, naming them Fish and Frog, but after a year Frog was again adopted, this time by a family of wolves. This adoption was contested, so it had to be brought before the Senate of Wolves, where it was ratified. When Frog grew up, he set about making a city for his people, but through a rash act his twin Fish was killed.

Rose: Red rose (147).

Burning Rose: Red Flower (150).

Now-Familiar Names: Meschia and Meschiane (151).

Myth: The legend of Romulus and Remus, from the founding of Rome, provides the basic structure of the tale. Juno is the queen "Early Summer," and according to Ovid's book *Fasti,* Juno used a magic flower to impregnate herself. Mars is "Spring Wind," Rhea Silvia is "Bird of the Wood," with Romulus as Frog and Remus as Fish.

Children's Literature: "Mowgli's Brothers" of Kipling's *The Jungle Book* (1894). Mowgli's name means "frog." "Black Killer" seems a lot like Mowgli's panther friend Bagheera. The Kipling story also has the wolf pack's meeting at Council Rock, where Bagheera buys the boy's life with a freshly killed bull.

Americana: With Squanto (157) we arrive at the first Thanksgiving (1621). Squanto was the last survivor of the Patuxet, a tribe wiped out by disease. He gave important aid to the *Mayflower* pilgrims, the most iconic being the planting of fish to grow the maize.

Harlan Ellison: Greg Feeley traces the detail "met in solemn conclave" (147-48) to Harlan Ellison's multiple award-winning story "'Repent,

Harlequin!' Said the Ticktockman" (1965) in his 1991 two-part article (*New York Review of Science Fiction No. 32,* p. 13).

20. The Circle of the Sorcerers

Severian and son stumble upon an arboreal village of sorcerers who deftly kidnap the boy.

Echo: Association of tunnel (161) links to mine at Saltus (II, chap. 5-6); memory intoxication (161) links to when Triskele lay dead (I, chap. 4).

21. The Duel of Magic

In order to win his son back, Severian must fight a magical duel with one of the sorcerers.

Paradoxes to Perfect Memory: Doeskin or human skin? The sack carrying the Claw is first described as being doeskin (III, chap. 1, 13), but here it is said to be "human skin" (III, chap. 21, 173). First flagged in 1983 in the book *Realms of Fantasy* (p. 120) by Edwards and Holdstock as a concrete example of how Wolfe uses careful signals to cast doubt upon Severian's memory.

Magical Effects: For the duel, Abundatius says, "You must weave your spells" (170-71). When little Severian calls Severian "Father," "it seemed to weaken the net Decuman was knotting around my mind" (173). This "netting" links to the water scenes in both the Gyoll (I, chap. 2) and the Lake of Birds (I, chap. 22), retroactively highlighting the magic in those cases.

Contrarian Severian: Abundantius says, "You may sit here, nearest the door . . . He will sit at the farther end" (170). Severian does the opposite, "Taking little Severian by the hand, I led him to the blind end of that dark place."

22. The Skirts of the Mountain

The magical duel is interrupted by the arrival of the blob-like slug, another one of Hethor's pets.

23. The Cursed Town

Severian and son escape the village and climb further up Mount Typhon. In the lap of the carved idol they find the cursed town, where buildings left over from the construction period stand waist-high to the giant automatons still milling about.

24. The Corpse

Investigating a central building, the pair discover the desiccated corpse of a two-headed man, but the boy is more curious about the gold ring on Mount

Typhon's finger, so they hike up there. As he touches the gold, little Severian is instantly killed by hidden energy weapons. Depressed nearly to the point of suicide, Severian sleeps in the cursed town.

Bible: The death of little Severian is like an unwitting sacrifice of Isaac (Genesis 22:1-12).

David Lindsay: This "little Severian" episode of seven chapters feels like something from *A Voyage to Arcturus* in that Severian takes up an orphaned son, successfully rescues him from some evil magic users and a terrible monster, only to have him suddenly snatched away.

25. Typhon and Piaton

When Severian wakes up the next morning he meets a living two-headed man, the corpse having been revived by the Claw. It is Monarch Typhon, a tyrant whose name has been forgotten for thousands of years. Typhon gets him into a boat-like elevator that starts off going downward for several minutes.

Jealousy: Severian admits to jealousy over the deep feeling of Dorcas for Jolenta as expressed by Dorcas after Jolenta died (201). This adds a revenge twist to his Jolenta tryst, in addition to lust and his contrarian nature.

Proust: The jealousy detail is very Proustian, since in *The Captive,* the Narrator obsesses over Albertine's various homosexual affairs with Lea, Mademoiselle Vinteuil, and Andrée.

Commentary: With the shuttlecock boat's movement we see a hint of the direction disorientation again, faintly like the up-down confusion in the drowning experience of both the river (I, chap. 2) and possibly in the Lake of Birds (I, between chapters 22 and 23).

26. The Eyes of the World

Typhon and Severian emerge in the head-chamber of the mountain. Typhon tries to tempt Severian with the throne of Urth, but Severian manages to kill him.

Jack Vance: The title is close to *The Eyes of the Overworld* (1966), the first Cugel novel, in which the "eyes" are essentially contact lenses that act as "rose-colored glasses," turning the mundane world into a place of wonder and delight for those who wear them.

James Blish: One detail echoes Blish's novel *Black Easter* (1968), which has the line regarding a demon, "It had women's breasts and an enormous erection, which it nursed alternately with hands folded into the gesture of benediction" (last few pages). Greg Feeley brings up this Blish-bit in his 1991 essay (*New York Review of Science Fiction No. 32,* p. 13-14).

Bible: The Temptation of Jesus is mentioned in three of the four gospels. "No mountain so high" (214) alludes to the Gospel of Matthew:

Again, the devil taketh him up into an exceeding high mountain, and showeth him all the kingdoms of the world, and the glory of them; And saith unto him, All these things will I give thee, if thou wilt fall down and worship me. (Matthew 4:8-9)

Apollo: In Greek myth Typhon and Python are two monsters associated with each other. Typhon was killed by Zeus, Python was killed by Apollo. Typhon and Python were very close, and Homer says Python was the nurse of Typhon. When Apollo killed Python he won the tripod triskele. Wolfe seems to be using this material, such that Piaton is the human form of Python.

David Lindsay: The Typhon episode of two chapters strikes me as being like something from *A Voyage to Arcturus* because Severian faces a Satanic figure, which happens a few times in Lindsay's book.

27. On High Paths

Descending the mountains, Severian comes to Lake Diuturna.

Americana: Severian's climb from the eye of the mountain idol, "the worst climb of my life" (216), seems an allusion to the scene in Hitchcock's feature film *North by Northwest* (1959), wherein the hero climbs down the carved face of Mount Rushmore, a monument completed in 1941.

Religion: A number of religious terms:

- Empyrian (219) a typo for Empyrean, the place in the highest heaven, supposedly the region of elemental fire. In Christian literature (e.g. Dante's *Paradiso)* it was used as the dwelling place of God.
- Amschaspands (220), the six Zoroastrian archangels. This builds upon the Zoroastrian elements of Dr. Talos's play, namely Meschia, Meschiane, and Jahi.
- The Ylem (220) is the primordial first substance from which the elements are formed, but Wolfe uses it here as an aspect of the Increate.
- The Theophany (221), visible manifestation of God.

Bible: The line "I now hold in my mind the experiences of so many men and women" (222) sounds like the man called "Legion" because he was possessed by so many spirits: "And he asked him, What is thy name? And he answered, saying, My name is Legion: for we are many" (Mark 5:9).

28. The Hetman's Dinner

Severian's attempt to intimidate the villagers into giving him free room and board backfires—he is drugged, and the Claw is taken away from him.

Bible: After the temptation, Jesus arrived at the Sea of Galilee, the body of water where he found his first disciples (Simon Peter, Andrew, John, and James).

Jack Vance: Severian's tactic with the hetman seems very much like something the rogue Cugel would perform. This is ironic, since Severian had just been remorseful about taking on airs with the sorcerers ("the memory of the lies I had told the magicians" (185)), and earlier his try at bullying an innkeeper had landed him in bed with Baldanders (I, chap. 15), a somewhat qualified success. That Severian is hoist by his own petard this time is an interesting release of the lofty, holy tension from "The Eyes of the World."

Commentary: From the cosmic horror of *A Voyage to Arcturus* to the roguish antics of Cugel is a precipitous drop that somehow discharges the tension without becoming bathetic.

29. The Hetman's Boat

The villagers begin to transport a bound Severian across the lake to the same dreaded tower to which they had sent the Claw.

Bible: The water with an alien shore is a match for the Sea of Galilee in Roman times, which had a Jewish side and a Gentile side. The Gentile side was the Decapolis, and this was the homeland of the man called Legion, mentioned before in notes to chapter 27.

30. Natrium

As floating islands close in on the hetman's boat, Severian seizes the opportunity to escape by splashing water onto the natrium slug thrower, destroying the boat in an explosion.

James Joyce: "Wandering Rocks" is episode 10 of *Ulysses* (1922). *Ulysses* is patterned after Homer's *Odyssey,* in which the wandering rocks are mentioned by the sorceress Circe, but they are located along the route that Odysseus avoided. (Joyce used his chapter as an excuse for vignettes of many different characters wandering through Dublin.) Despite all that, here, through Severian's action, the mythological scenario is played out: the wandering rocks appear; they close in on the ship; the ship is broken up.

31. The People of the Lake

Rescued by the islanders and determined to retrieve the Claw, Severian plans an assault on the strange tower which happens to look like a toadstool since a flying saucer is hovering over it.

Myth: The islanders worship Oannes (251), a Babylonian god half-man, half-fish. Oannes appeared from the sea and taught humans important things for one day before returning to the sea. He reappeared a few times over thousands of years; one time was to warn Utnapishtim, the Babylonian Noah, about the coming flood.

A Secret of the Guild: "And the secret [imparted to me by Master Palaemon and Master Gurloes just before I was elevated] is only that we torturers obey. . . . No one truly obeys unless he will do the unthinkable in obedience; no one will do the unthinkable save we" (252).

32. To the Castle

When Severian knocks at the gate in an attempt to bluff his authority as lictor of Thrax, he is surprised to see Doctor Talos open the door and welcome him in.

Paradoxes to Perfect Memory: Dorcas or Cyriaca? Severian writes that Dorcas told him of the flying saucer (257), but the text shows us Cyriaca telling him that (III, chap. 12, 90).

Dickens: The door knocker shaped "like the head of a man" (258), evokes a detail from "A Christmas Carol" (1843) concerning the door of Scrooge, "And then let any man explain to me, if he can, how it happened that Scrooge, having his key in the lock of the door, saw in the knocker . . . not a knocker, but Marley's face."

Wolf: Howling of a wolf (259), actually an insane person, one of many prisoners in the tower.

33. Ossipago, Barbatus, and Famulimus

Inside the tower, Baldanders and Talos are involved in delicate negotiations with three aliens or "hierodules" over super science knowledge and/or artifacts. Severian is first baffled by the hierodules because they seem to know him, then he is shocked to learn that Doctor Talos is a homunculus created by Baldanders.

New Detail of Past Event: Ossipago, Barbatus, and Famulimus were at the play at the House Absolute (II, chap. 24), and they shot Baldanders when he went berserk (II, chap. 25). Likely they were the only hierodules there.

Christopher Marlowe: There is something about Doctor Talos and the three hierodules that hints at Marlowe's Doctor Faustus dealing with his devils in *The Tragical History of the Life and Death of Doctor Faustus* (1592). Closer to the target, Marlowe's Faustus raised Helen of Troy, and Talos, through some sort of mesmerism, got the drab waitress possessed by a "Helen" as well (since Saint Jolenta is also known as Helen of Poland).

Myth: That Talos is a man-created creature is hinted in his name, because Talos was a metal man fashioned by Hephaestus/Vulcan in Greco-Roman myth. This is mentioned by Wolfe in "Onomastics, the Study of Names" (*Castle of Days*, 253-54).

Jack Vance: The detail of Talos's synthetic nature is a second point of similarity he shares with T'sais of *The Dying Earth,* along with striking heads off flowers. The fact that Baldanders made Talos puts Baldanders in the role of Pandelume, the great sorcerer Turjan of Miir seeks.

34. Masks

Baldanders reveals that he came first and was a small man at that time, then he created Talos. Ossipago states that Baldanders must grow to stay young. Severian asks for the return of the Claw, and the visiting hierodules ask to see it. They are not impressed. The hierodules reveal some details about themselves, but they also give Severian an enigmatic test which he fails. They leave without giving Baldanders any gifts.

Animal Form: Baldanders complains the hierodules treat him like "a bear on a chain" (269).

Madeleine L'Engle: The hierodules Osspago, Barbatus, and Famulimus bear a certain resemblance to the trio Mrs. Whatsit, Mrs. Who, and Mrs. Which of the young adult novel *A Wrinkle in Time* (1962). Both trios are angel-like and masked. Even Severian's surprise when the trio bows to him finds a parallel near the end of *A Wrinkle in Time* with this line: "Mr. Murry took a step forward and bowed [to the trio], and to [his daughter] Meg's amazement the three ladies bowed back to him" (chapter 12).

35. The Signal

The hierodules's ship takes off. Baldanders, in fury that Severian's superstition has cost him new knowledge, throws the Claw from the top of the tower. The islanders, having been waiting for a sign from Severian, launch their attack.

Mary Shelley: "The castle? The monster? The man of learning? I only just thought of it" (277). This is a semi-veiled allusion to *Frankenstein* (1818), a novel that is a contender for the title of first true science fiction story, its main rival being *The Time Machine* (1895) by H. G. Wells.

H. G. Wells: The flying saucer hovering over Baldanders's castle is actually, surprisingly, a time machine.

36. The Fight in the Bailey

Severian fights his way down, while the islanders fight their way up.

37. *Terminus Est*

Severian's sword is destroyed in the fight, and Baldanders escapes by diving into the lake.

Tarot: The image of Baldanders swooping down (288) offers a parallel to the tarot card The Tower.

Validation of the Vision Dream: The battle scene echoes the toy puppet play (I, chap. 15, 141-42).

Borges: When Baldanders takes to the water, we reveal that the "Baldanders" entry in *The Book of Imaginary Beings* says the character ultimately derives from Proteus; and we add that Homer called Proteus the "Old Man of the Sea."

38. The Claw

The next day Severian searches for the Claw, and finds amid the broken glass of its outer case the heart of the jewel—a black claw. The Claw of the Conciliator was never really a gem at all; it was this dark object encased in pretty blue glass. Severian leaves the lake, heading north.

King Arthur: When Severian casts the sword (remnant) into the lake, he mimics the return of Excalibur to its lake when King Arthur is at the brink of death.

Philosophy: A complicated passage:

Just as summer-killed meat draws flies, so the court draws spurious sages, philosophists, and acosmists who remain there as long as their purses and their wits will maintain them . . . At sixteen or so, Thecla was attracted . . . to their lectures on theogony, thodicy, and the like, and I recall one particularly in which a phoebad put forward as an ultimate truth the ancient sophistry of the existence of three Adonai, that of the city (or of the people), that of the poets, and that of the philosophers. (295)

Definitions of Unusual Terms
- Philosophist: Usually a derogatory term for a philosopher of what is held to be erroneous speculation or philosophy.
- Acosmist: One who denies the existence of the universe, or of a universe as distinct from God.
- Theogony: The geneology of a group of gods.
- Thodicy: A typo for "theodicy," vindication of divine goodness in view of the existence of evil.
- Phoebad: Technically this word should probably be "phoebas," a priestess of Apollo. It looks like a back formation from the plural "phoebades," or a simple typo.
- Three Adonai: Where "Adonai" is a Hebrew name for God, at first this seems like it might relate to the Christian Trinity (Father, Son, and Holy Spirit), but then it breaks instead along

62

lines of social class (the people, the poets, and the philosophers), sounding like something from Socrates. Since Socrates himself felt Apollo was the specific god who had guided him to his wisdom, which seems related to the "phoebas" of the passage, let us imagine a distinct Apollo for the people, another for the poets, and a third for the philosophers.

The next two paragraphs continue this thread:

Might it not be, she asked . . . , that instead of traveling, as has always been supposed, down three roads to the same destination, they are actually traveling toward three quite different ones? After all, when in common life we behold three roads issuing from the same crossing, we do not assume they all proceed toward the same goal.

I found (and find) this suggestion as rational as it is repellent, and it represents for me all that monomaniacal fabric of argument, so tightly woven that not even the tiniest objection or spark of light can escape its net, in which human minds become enmeshed whenever the subject is one in which no appeal to fact is possible. (295-96)

The argument seems to be going along Socratic paths. In Book II of Plato's *Republic*, Socrates states that in myths of the gods told by both commoners and poets, the gods were depicted as quarrelsome and vindictive, too much like humans. Socrates, a philosopher, complained that the real gods must be just and honest. That is, to Socrates there were three versions of the gods, but two of them were wrong in the same way. So we might say that the civic Apollo is a rapist and a source of disease; that the poetic Apollo tells lies and uses seduction; whereas only the philosopher's Apollo is good.

Bible: The term "Tetrarchic ring" (296) is another veiled reference pointing to the Sea of Galilee, which at the time of Jesus was bordered by the Tetrarchy of Philip, the Tetrarchy of Antipas, and the Decapolis. This finds congruence with Lake Diuturna's shore being divided among three distinct groups: the village Murene, the villas of the exultants, and the tower of Baldanders.

Historically the Herodian Tetrarchy was formed after the death of Herod the Great in 4 BC. His kingdom of Judea was divided between his four heirs: son Herod Archelaus as ethnarch, sons Herod Antipas and Philip as tetrarchs in inheritance, with his sister Salome ruling the district of Jamnia. (Note the term "ethnarch," which is used twice in *Sword of the Lictor,* first as an exultant title (III, chap. 2, 19), then as a presumed figure ruling the area of Lake Diuturna (III, chap. 29, 235).)

Appendix: A Note on Provincial Administration

Wolfe tells of archons and tetrarchs, clavigers and dimarchi.

VOLUME IV: THE CITADEL OF THE AUTARCH

At two o'clock in the morning, if you open your window and listen,
You will hear the feet of the Wind that is going to call the sun.
And the trees in the shadow rustle and the trees in the moonlight glisten,
And though it is deep, dark night, you feel that the night is done.

[sic]–Rudyard Kipling

Epigraph: This quote comes from the very beginning of Rudyard Kipling's "The Dawn Wind" (*Castle of Days*, 230). The poem was first published in *A School History of England* (1911) by C. R. L. Fletcher and Rudyard Kipling, where it was used to close chapter 6, "The End of the Middle Ages."

1. The Dead Soldier

A few weeks after leaving Lake Diuturna, Severian stumbles upon the body of a soldier who had died of disease while deployed against Vodalus's rebels.

Milton: "Just as our familiar Urth holds such monstrosities as Erebus, Abaia, and Arioch" (9). While Arioch is a Biblical figure of a mortal king (Genesis 14:1, 9), this allusion, mentioned in association with Erebus and Abaia, is more specifically a named demon in Milton's *Paradise Lost* (1667). Here is his only mention in that poem:

> Nor stood unmindful Abdiel to annoy
> The atheist crew, but with redoubled blow
> Ariel, and Arioch, and the violence
> Of Ramiel, scorched and blasted, overthrew.

(Book 6, lines 369-72)

To give context to the quote: "Abdiel" is a good angel attacking the fallen angels Ariel, Arioch, and Ramiel. "Abdiel" is a mortal name in the Bible; "Ariel" is a mortal name in Biblical Hebrew but also an occult angel; "Ramiel" is a fallen angel in the Book of Enoch.

Michael Moorcock: Within the modern fantasy genre, Arioch is famous as a duke of Hell and patron to "the White Wolf" Elric of Melniboné, beginning with "The Dreaming City" (1961).

Animal: Smilodon tracks (11).

Thematic Echo: The soldier's epistle rattling across the moss (15) is akin to the notules "rustling" in the treetops as Severian and Jonas fled (II, chap. 12, 105).

Stephan Crane: Severian's finding of the corpse is something like that signature scene in *The Red Badge of Courage* (1895):

> He was being looked at by a dead man who was seated with his back against a columnlike tree. . . . The eyes, staring at the youth, had changed to the dull hue to be seen on the side of dead fish. . . . Over the gray skin of the face ran little ants. (*The Red Badge of Courage,* Chap. 7, near end)

This passage seems to echo a part earlier in Severian's narrative, where he described Jonas in the antechamber: "Now he [Jonas] slumped against the wall just as I have since seen a corpse sit with its back to a tree" (II, chap. 16, 137). So the slumped-Jonas detail seems to foreshadow the dead soldier in the woods.

However, when Severian is going through the woods, avoiding soldiers, he sees a fly "settle on a brown object projecting from behind one of the thronging trees. A boot" (IV, chap. 1, 13). Based on the aforementioned model of "slumped Jonas," one might expect this boot to be "toe up," but Severian's further examination shows, "He lay sprawled, with one leg crumpled under him and the other extended" (14). He might be face up, or more likely face down, but the corpse is never propped up against the tree.

So it is a big authorial fake out: this corpse is not the one alluded to in the "slumped Jonas" quote.

2. The Living Soldier

Severian uses the Claw on the corpse and it revives. Together they walk out of the forest.

Claw Notes: He puts it in the corpse's mouth first, then pricks the corpse's forehead (17); there is a rustling as if the spirit is walking back to the body (18).

Untraced Echo: The line "like incense it rose . . . suggesting something I could not quite recall" (19) seems a link to the incense-like aroma of the burning tree when the Claw revived the uhlan (II, chap. 13, 103).

Echo: A medley (19) touching on the beginning of volume I; Dorcas's words at the lake, about the last thing she remembered (I, chap. 23, 204) and a line she gave in the play, in the role of Meschiane (II, chap. 24, 218).

Rose: Purple roses of the necropolis (20).

Women: "Dorcas belonged, as I now realized, to that vast group of women (which may, indeed include all women) who betray us—and to that special type who betray us not for some present rival but for their own pasts" (20). In the 1986 *Interzone* interview, Elliott Swanson asked about this line, and Wolfe responded: "I think Severian means that men want to be loved more than any other thing is loved, and that though they may occasionally attract such love, they never have the power to hold it" (Wright, *Shadows of the New Sun*, 76-77).

Religion: Severian recalls Thecla mentioning a god Caitanya (21). A Hindu mystic of this name was regarded by his followers as an incarnation of both Krishna and his consort Radha in a single body.

Echo: The corpse's coutel (21-22) and Agia's dagger (III, chap. 16, 123).

Commentary: The strange vagueness regarding the position of the corpse noted in the previous chapter might be another expression of Severian's up/down confusion in the presence of magic. This becomes plausible only after the resurrection of the soldier.

3. Through Dust

Severian and the soldier follow the road, looking for the army.

Enigma: The razor detail (23-24).

Sidelong Glance Reveals the Unseen: A hint of Jonas through profile (25), a thematic echo to Jolenta near her end (II, chap. 29, 269).

Time-bending of the Claw: "[B]ent the moment to one when they [the wounds] would be nearly healed" (27) means time accelerated. And Severian had just said of Dorcas "Her hair was long before she cut it" (27).

4. Fever

Severian and the soldier find a lazaret, this one a medical tent maintained near the front by the Pelerines. Severian succumbs to fever-driven vision dreams.

Apollo: This sun-god is also a deity of disease. It is curious that Severian catches the contagion, almost as if he is taking it from Jonas and fighting it for both of them in his body.

Americana: That the Pelerines are acting as medics at the front finds historical resonance with the various "nuns of the battlefield" who served during the American Civil War.

Dream: Severian wakes in apprentice dorm (33). Malrubius's sick room in Typhon's head chamber, with Cumaean, Merryn, and Thecla (34). Hethor in water carafe (35). Malrubius and Triskele (36).

5. The Lazaret

After the fever breaks, Severian meets fellow patients Foila (an armigette), Melito (a farmboy soldier), Hallvard (a seal hunter turned soldier), and Loyal to the Group of Seventeen (an Ascian prisoner). Severian learns about Correct Thought and Approved Texts.

Thematic Echo: Recovering in the lazaret like the first time after the duel (I, chap. 28).

6. Miles, Foila, Melito, and Hallvard

Miles, the resurrected soldier, is somehow also Jonas returned from the mirrors, two souls in one body searching for Jolenta, Jonas's true love. But when Severian tells him that Jolenta has died, Miles/Jonas wanders off in a daze.

Meanwhile, patients Melito and Hallvard both want to marry Foila, so she decides they will have a story-telling contest for which Severian, as an outsider, shall be the judge.

Onomastics: Severian gives the amnesia-suffering soldier the name "Miles," which is Latin for "soldier."

7. Hallvard's Story—The Two Sealers

Hallvard tells his story about sealers.

Hallvard's bachelor uncles Anskar and Gundulf shared a boat and an inheritance from Hallvard's grandfather. One day Anskar returned alone from fishing, saying his brother had been dragged under by a harpooned seal, but some days later Gundulf's body washed ashore with evidence of murder. Anskar confessed he killed his brother in an argument over a young woman.

Commentary: More Viking material. "It is about the intense passion the men of his people have for their women, a dedication that verges on madness" (*Lexicon Urthus*).

Genre: Weird Tale/True Crime.

Melito Notes: Suitor has prospects of inheriting property.

Analysis: While the story sounds like the stuff of Icelandic Sagas, the closest match is a distortion of Saint Hallvard's death. In 1043 this young Norwegian offered refuge on his ship to a pregnant woman pursued by three men claiming her to be a thief. The woman was probably a thrall, being a slave or a servant. The three men killed both the woman and Saint Hallvard with arrows. They buried her on the beach and tried to sink his corpse in the sea with a millstone, but miraculously his body refused to sink and their crimes were thereby revealed.

In "Two Sealers," uncle Gundulf loves a young widow who is an outcast: "no man would have her because she had borne a child by a man who had died the winter before" (58). Gundulf is the murderer, and the victim is uncle Anskar. Anskar means "spear of God," and it is Hallvard's makeshift spear that reveals the beached "seal" is really the dead uncle, in a way that hints at shapeshifting. Gundulf later bellows like a bull seal (57).

8. The Pelerine

In the evening, Severian meets a Pelerine who has been in the order for thirty years. He tries to return the Claw to her, but she is skeptical of his claims to have resurrected the dead with it and refuses to believe that the talon or unguis he shows her is somehow the heart of the gem she remembers.

9. Melito's Story—The Cock, the Angel, and the Eagle

The next day, Melito tells his tale.

A rooster rose through the ranks of fighting to the point where he successfully defeated an owl trying to snatch his sweetheart. This singular victory led him to boasting that he could beat any feathered thing, which brought the attention of an angel. The cock tried to talk his way out of the fight, but then in exasperation the angel sent an eagle, who beat the boaster nearly to death, yet the rooster maintained his dignity, thereby eking a victory from apparent defeat.

Commentary: The story seems a clever blend of at least two separate tales. There is an emphasis on cleverness in both the animal hero and the human teller. Shape-shifting is named as an ability of angels, but only a minor character actually shifts form.

Genre: Farmyard fable.

Aesop: "The Fighting Cocks and the Eagle" begins when two roosters fight to rule the farmyard. The beaten one seeks shelter, the victor prances around, boasting. An eagle, seeing the victor, swoops down and takes him away for dinner. The beaten one emerges as the true winner.

But notice how Wolfe adds backstory context through telling first about the eccentric farmer: "The farmer . . . had a great many strange ideas about farming" (67) leads to three paragraphs about why he allowed his roosters to fight.

Bible: "Wrestling with an angel" describes Jacob (Genesis 32:22-32).

Hallvard Notes: Suitor plays on a woman's sympathy for wounded hero.

Melito's Rebuttal: It is the worst story he knows.

Hallvard's Counterpoint: This is a contest of stories told, not stories that have not been heard.

Loyal to the Group of Seventeen's Comment: Judging should be on style rather than content (73).

10. Ava

In the evening, Severian meets Ava, a postulant (an apprentice of the Pelerines) originally from an optimate family living in the Sanguinary Field area of Nessus. She had witnessed his duel with Agilus but does not recognize him as the "exultant in masquerade" she remembers fighting Agilus. Having heard about Severian's "delusions" from the Pelerine, Ava is also skeptical at first, but gradually she comes to quietly believe.

Animal Form: The postulant Ava reminds Severian of the tame deer in the Autarch's garden (76). This links to when Severian had his fling with Jolenta (II, chap. 23, 203).

Twin Talk: Severian says, "If I do [have a twin], she's a witch" (79).

New Detail of Past Event: The leader of the Pelerines had the cathedral burned (83).

11. Loyal to the Group of Seventeen's Story—The Just Man

The next day the Ascian prisoner enters the story-telling contest with a tale made up of quotes from Authorized Texts. It is translated by Foila.

Once there was a collective farm where one good man was cheated by all the others. When he complained, they beat him, so he went to the capital and complained to the authorities. Upon his return to the farm, he was beaten again. He went to the capital again and complained directly to the authorities. The authorities told him to evict the others from the farm in their name. He tried this, but the others mocked him and beat him again. The man returned to the capital a third time and became a beggar. This time the authorities told him they would put the others in prison. The man returned to the farm and was beaten again. Once more he went to the capital, and now the bad men were afraid. They abandoned the farm and were never seen again. The man returned and enjoyed his life at the farm.

What's Her Game: Severian wonders at the motive of Foila as translator (90): Was it just mischief? Was it a real interest in the man? Or was it interest in the military information she might draw from him?

Commentary: Enduring trials while seeking justice.

Genre: Fable.

Severian's Note: The story signals that the teller "would never give up" (90).

Bible: Psalm 37 seems an appropriate model. It begins "Fret not thyself of evildoers" and five times repeats words to the effect that the meek shall inherit the earth or the land (Psalm 37: 9; 11; 22; 29; 34).

12. Winnoc

Severian meets Winnoc, a slave of the Pelerines. Winnoc was originally from Nessus, and thirty years before had been whipped by Journeyman Palaemon, who had himself been exiled from the torturers' guild for some crime. Shortly after this punishment, Winnoc sold himself to the Pelerines.

Commentary: Winnoc witnessed Palaemon in exile (92-95). This was perhaps ten years before Severian was born (99).

13. Foila's Story—The Armiger's Daughter

Foila tells a story, entering the contest with a magical tale about an armigette with three suitors.

The armigette releases her brown bird and says she will marry the one who shows her the bird again. The first suitor wounds the brown rider; the second suitor tries to trick and kill the brown rider; and the third suitor goes along with the brown rider. The brown rider turns out to be the armigette after all, and she marries the third suitor.

Commentary: Clever and reflecting, with a shape-changing heroine and a shifting point of view that maintains her secrets. It seems like a straightforward adventure story, albeit one that mirrors the teller's situation, but ultimately it has a surprising literary pedigree.

In her story, the first suitor wounds the brown rider (103), and Foila's first suitor, Hallvard, told a story about killing for love. The second suitor tries to trick the brown rider (105), and Melito told a story about trickery. The third suitor goes along with the brown rider (106), and Loyal to the Group of Seventeen told a story about persistence and endurance.

Japanese Poem: Japanese school children learn a simple poem to remember the traits of the three warlords who sought to unify Japan: Nobunaga, Hideyoshi, and Tokugawa.

"If a bird won't sing, kill it." (Nobunaga)
"If a bird won't sing, coax it." (Hideyoshi)
"If a bird won't sing, wait for it." (Tokugawa)

Bible: A bit of "prodigal son" in reverse, as she comes home in glory.

Echo: The line "food for him, clean water, and safety" (108) sounds like a phrase from "The Just Man" (IV, chap. 11, 86), but maybe it is gentle mockery, since it refers to a pet bird in a cage and the Ascian line is about workers on a farm.

Further Commentary: Her story implies that Foila would choose Loyal. Again we ponder her motives. The complications of her marrying a prisoner of war are probably so great that, if Loyal is declared the winner, Foila is still effectively free. If Foila is declared winner, she is free. So Foila has stacked the deck in her favor, raising a 33% chance of winning to 50%.

14. Mannea

In the evening, Severian hides the Claw in the altar of the Pelerines. He is approached by Chatelaine Mannea, the highest-ranking Pelerine currently at the lazaret, who asks him to undertake an urgent mission to fetch an anchorite (holy hermit) from a hermitage that is about to be overrun by Ascians. Severian agrees to the job.

Echo: Casting his memory back to a time he had felt so well before leads to the morning he had met Agia (110), linking to that chapter (I, chap. 16); these memories lead to a prayer of reflection and confession (111); and the returning of the Claw (112).

Bible: Severian's relief, his joy, the "new creation" and birth (113) seems like a link to the following scripture, "If we confess our sins, he is faithful and just to forgive us [our] sins, and to cleanse us from all unrighteousness" (1 John 1:9); "Being born again, not of corruptible seed, but of incorruptible, by the word of God, which liveth and abideth forever" (1 Peter 1:23).

Thematic Echo: When Mannea touches Severian and he feels as if he were brushed "by the wing of a bird" (115), it evokes Jader's sister in the jacal after being healed: "I know you are only the wing of some poor bird" (III, chap. 8, 67).

15. The Last House

With safe-conduct in hand, Severian walks the twenty leagues to the Last House. Despite his shortcuts, it takes exactly as long as Mannea told him it would take—two days.

Disorientation as a Sign of Magic: Severian experiences some up/down disorientation (119).

Echo: Apprehension about being targeted (119) links back to Agia's assassins (II, chap. 7, 59-60). Association (120) links back to the jungle hut (I, chap. 21), where the missionaries are now husband and wife (120), before brother and sister (II, chap. 31, 294), even though Marie had identified Robert as her husband (I, chap. 21, 189).

16. The Anchorite

Severian meets the anchorite Master Ash, and sleeps upstairs at the hermitage, known as the Last House.

Untraced Allusion: Talk of a story of a man who sold his shadow (125) and traveled with a man who had no reflection (126).

Warfare: Ash lists three reasons for sudden strength: a new alliance, the termination of another war, or the need for immediate victory (127).

17. Ragnarok—The Final Winter

In the morning, Severian looks out the window onto a world covered in ice—the Ragnarok future. He figures out the time-bending architecture of the Last House, where each floor exists in a different geological era. Following Mannea's instructions, he drags Master Ash out of the hermitage. Ash disappears and presumably the Ragnarok timeline implodes.

Myth: Ragnarok is the Norse "Doom of the Gods," a time when the forces of light and darkness clash for a final battle that annihilates both sides.

Places with Strange Time: The Botanic Gardens, where time never changes in the lake; where time moves forward or backward in the jungle (132).

Double Echo: When Severian writes, "I seemed to hear the beating of a drum" (135) this links back to the drum used to advertise the green man during his captivity (II, chap. 3, 25), but it also has a chance resemblance to the mystic drumbeat heard at key moments of Lindsay's *A Voyage to Arcturus*.

Commentary: That Master Ash is an "anchorite," or hermit, is punningly played as him being an anchor for the Ragnarok future.

Myth: A hint of Sumerian Gilgamesh and Utnapishtim with the loaves of bread (chap. 16, 125) and sleeping. More specifically, in *The Epic of Gilgamesh*, when Gilgamesh arrived at the house of Utnapishtim (the Babylonian Noah, who lived beyond the edge of the world), he was so exhausted that he slept for a number of days. When he woke, he could not believe the claims of his host that he had slept for such a long time, so Utnapishtim showed him the seven loaves of daily bread set beside him as he slept, with the first one stale and the seventh still in the cooking embers. Thus Gilgamesh suffered a time displacement while visiting an immortal who had survived vast disaster.

18. Foila's Request

Upon his return to the lazaret, Severian finds that the whole area has been razed in an Ascian attack. After following the trail of survivors, he manages to find Foila who tells him the others are probably dead. Her dying wish is that he remember the stories, so he writes them down onto the blank pages of the brown book.

Myth: Ash and Vine (139) are the Adam and Eve of Norse mythology. They are similar to Meschia and Meschiane who grew from a tree.

Paradoxes to Perfect Memory: Severian, writing about the Atrium of Time, gives the detail about the "obelisk covered with sundials" (140). This is in high contrast to the first description (I, chap. 4, 42).

Echo: Talking to Master Ash about the day of Triskele (140-41) offers another version of that time (I, chap. 4); raises the event to a resurrection, a retroactive miracle; as if Severian "had the Claw already" (141), which paradoxes the Claw.

Echo: Severian notes he had killed a bull once with his sword (141), linking to that time on the pampas (II, chap. 29, 270).

19. Guasacht

Severian spends two days wandering, then joins Guasacht's troop, the Eighteenth Bacele of the Irregular Contarii.

Falchion Note: This is Severian's second falchion (146), the first being the one he took from the dead soldier (chap. 1, 14).

Religious Term: Severian writes "(if it be the will of Apeiron)" (147). This is a philosophical term from ancient Greece, a "primal principle of all matter" similar to "the Ylem" used in the previous volume (III, chap. 27, 220).

Bible: Severian's fusion with Thecla produces a "new man" (147), with parallels to scripture: "Therefore if any man be in Christ, he is a new creature: old things are passed away; behold, all things are become new" (2 Corinthians 5:17).

Little Red Riding Hood: Daria, with her fox-colored hair (151) and her riding crops, seems a surprising manifestation of the fairytale heroine.

Language of Flowers: Daria and calambac (153); a fragrant wood, such as agalloch.

20. Patrol

Sometime later, Guasacht's group finds an armored coach of the Autarch, bearing gold and mastiff-man guards, bogged down in the mud and harassed by Ascian soldiers. Guasacht's forces pin down the Ascians, but a new mob of treasure-seeking camp followers threatens to overwhelm them all, so a desperate alliance is formed between the mastiff-men, the irregulars, and the Ascians. Once they break out, the irregulars blast the Ascians, but before they can loot the coach themselves a squadron of anpiels arrives to preserve the gold for the Autarch.

Commentary: A combat story where enemies must cooperate.

Echo: The mob's weaponry is compared to that of the volunteers in the necropolis (155), a link to the beginning of volume I; the pistols (162) link to the attack on the hierodules (II, chap. 25); the anpiel (163) is linked to Melito's fable (IV, chap. 9).

21. Deployment

The Eighteenth Bacele is deployed at the frontlines.

Echo: Metaphor of army coming together (166) links to the stone town dust forming into beings (II, chap. 31).

Commentary: Perhaps another *Red Badge of Courage* point: "Fear is like one of those diseases that disfigures the face" (169). Then there is the whore angle

(170): Daria is fighting a slightly different internal battle, since she can elect to avoid combat in a way that Severian cannot.

22. Battle

Severian is wounded during the Third Battle of Orithyia.

Stephan Crane: At the war's front Severian sees corpses among trees, including "one who had contrived in dying to hook the collar of his . . . jacket to a splinter protruding from one of the broken trunks" (171), but this does not seem to match the slumped Jonas/tree leaning model (mentioned in notes for chapter 1), either.

Lewis Carroll: Chess is a part of *Through the Looking Glass,* and this chapter has chess and Wonderland touches.

Severian refers to "the squares of the checkerboard" (176), and later notes, "Watching it from a distance, I recalled my own thoughts of battle as a game of chess, and I felt that somewhere someone else had entertained the same thoughts and unconsciously allowed them to shape his plan" (177).

Allies and enemies are Wonderland-strange. The Daughters of War, an ally group, seem to be elephantine "rook" pieces, charging in straight lines. The dwarfish riders of tall men, an enemy group, seem like a nightmare version of knights. Then there is "a machine like a tower walking" (183), which echoes back to the Saltus Mine (II, chap. 6, 55).

23. The Pelagic Argosy Sights Land

After the battle, Severian is found and rescued by the Autarch.

Wolf: A dire wolf howls (184); another one (185).

Competing Zodiacs: At the end of the chapter, Severian starts talking to the Bull Constellation, admitting that he does not know his own zodiac sign, but then it seems Thecla remembers her sign is the Swan.

The sign of the Bull is our Taurus (April 21 to May 21), but the Swan is tricky, since our constellation Cygnus (Swan) cannot be part of the Zodiac. Instead Thecla's sign might be the Swan (September 2 to 29) from the Celtic Zodiac of thirteen signs, or it might be the Egyptian version of Sagittarius: "Dupuis said that [Sagittarius] was shown in Egypt as an Ibis or Swan" (Allen, *Star Names,* 353). Regardless, it makes sense that the exultants would have their own exclusive zodiac.

24. The Flier

The Autarch takes Severian aloft in a flier.

Echo: Memory (192) links to visiting the House Azure (I, chap. 9); thoughts on the echopraxia links to playing multiple parts in Talos's play (I, chap. 32).

Autarch's Roles and Titles: Third bursar (193); the "Legion" title used by woman-cats for the Autarch (196) pays out on the "My name is Legion" association previously made (II, chap. 27, 222).

Animal Form: Autarch as thrush (194); cat claw like the naked Claw (195).

25. The Mercy of Agia

The flier is shot down and the Autarch is wounded. Severian and the Autarch are captured by Ascians, but then the Ascians are wiped out by Vodalarii mounted on airborne monsters summoned by Hethor and commanded by Agia.

Echo: Mentioning the dead woman of the necropolis (208) links to the opening chapter (I, chap. 1); "Once I had imagined such creatures threshing . . ." (208) reaches back to a lover's revenge fantasy that ends with mercy (IV, chap. 2, 19-20).

The Cross: Severian looks for this constellation of the southern sky (209).

Paradox of the Vision Dream: The flying mount (211) links to the dream in Baldanders's bed (I, chap. 15, 139-40), but this time Severian is held by the monster, rather than riding it. This difference might suggest that in the vision Severian commanded the peryton; which implies Hethor as ally; which implies Agia as ally.

26. Above the Jungle

Severian and the Autarch are taken to Vodalus's base, an ancient ziggurat in the jungle. For payment, Agia wants to be allowed to kill Severian, but Vodalus refuses.

Thematic Echo: The jungle ziggurat (212) has a link to Talos's play, where Second Demon, speaking to Autarch, says, "Our travels but lately took us to the northern jungles, and there, in a temple older than man . . . we spoke to an ancient shaman who foretold great peril to your realm" (II, chap. 24, 225).

Principle of Primitivity: *Because the prehistoric cultures endured for so many chiliads, they have shaped our heritage in such a way as to cause us to behave as if their conditions obtained today* (217).

Echo: Re-reading "The Tale of the Student and His Son" (218) links to that chapter (II, chap. 17).

27. Before Vodalus

Vodalus had been expecting to capture the Autarch but does not recognize his old House Absolute spy as the Autarch, instead suspecting that Severian might be the one. Severian tells him the Autarch escaped.

Animal: Blood bat (220). The trail of this creature through the text is remarkable. The first mention was by Dorcas, who said, "Well, you did look like a black bat bending over me" (I, chap. 34, 288). Then she brought it up a volume later, saying, "I remember being told that there were blood bats farther north" (II, chap. 28, 266). Then Hildegrin reacts to their suggestion regarding the wounds of Jolenta by saying, "And a bat bite did it?" (II, chap. 31, 286). Severian directly tells little Severian, "[A] friend of mine was bitten by a blood bat once" (III, chap. 18, 145).

Jack Vance: At this late stage Vodalus reveals that he is analogous to Liane the Wayfarer, troubadour-bandit of *The Dying Earth.*

28. On the March

Severian and the Autarch are marched toward an Ascian camp.

Frame Tale: Today the last before I am to leave (225).

Echo: Frame-tale ritual of reduced gravity (226) links to the night above Thrax when he feared falling up (III, chap. 13, 100); three savage guides (228) link to the Jungle Garden (I, chap. 20-21).

29. Autarch of the Commonwealth

At the Ascian camp they are questioned by Ascian commanders in radio contact with their superiors. The Autarch, near death from his wounds, convinces Severian to become the new Autarch by taking a powerful dose of the analeptic alzabo, then killing the Autarch and eating his brain. Severian obeys.

Myth: The three Ascian women, looking at each other, seem like Norns (232).

Thematic Echo: When the Autarch says, "We hold humankind stationary [. . .] in barbarism" (236), he answers the theme of Jonas in the antechamber regarding the relatively short middle ages and this Age of the Autarch in which "It endured too long" (II, chap. 16, 137).

Commentary: Father Inire is with the insurgents (234-35), strong hint he is the "shaman."

Thematic Echo: "Are you all right?" (238) links up to Severian being memory-drunk when the cultellarii arrived at Saltus (II, chap. 8).

30. The Corridors of Time

Severian is rescued by Agia and the Green Man. Agia has killed Vodalus and now leads the rebellion herself. Before leaving him, the Green Man summons a small flying boat for him. On this ship the aquastor Malrubius answers many questions as they fly south, but Severian holds back on giving details at this point.

Echo: Hallucination (239) links to walking down the Adamnian Steps (I, chap. 19, 172); then the jade bust leads to the tent of the green man (II, chap.

3, 25); the crooked dagger in the shutter (240) from Casdoe's cabin (III, chap. 16, 123).

Autarch: Life as a boy in the kitchens (241).

Green Man: Other time questors, I will send two (242). Malrubius and Triskele.

Mazes: "It was a maze, but I was the owner and even the builder of that maze, with the print of my thumb on every passageway" (243). This alludes to the Naviscaput of "The Tale of the Student and His Son" (II, chap. 17), but it casts Severian as the monster. It also raises the suggestion of his own future self as being the stage manager above others.

The Second Timeship: Implied to be a saucer, like the one at Baldanders's castle. But it has gunwales (242).

31. The Sand Garden

Severian is dropped off on the beach where the River Gyoll meets the sea, and there he brushes a rose bush. A thorn breaks off in his skin. He recognizes it as the Claw.

The Second Timeship: The vehicle has rigging (245), so it seems less like a saucer and more like a watercraft. Its range for projecting aquastors "is but a few thousand years" (251), so it has moved that far away.

Thematic Echo: Malrubius's eyes were two more such stars (247), like Hethor's eyes as stars (III, chap. 13, 99).

Echo: Tracks of a two-wheeled cart (252) links back to the Sand Garden (I, chap. 19, 177).

Language of Flowers: The white rose of the bush on beach (252) means "I am worthy of you."

Bible: "[T]hat I might not walk shod on holy ground" (253) alludes to Moses and the burning bush, where God spoke to Moses, "And he said, Draw not nigh hither: put off thy shoes from off thy feet, for the place whereon thou standest is holy ground" (Exodus 3:5).

Burning Rose: The melding of a literal rose bush with an allusion to the burning bush gives another burning rose image.

32. The *Samru*

Severian catches a ride on the *Samru,* a ship heading up river. At his request they drop him off for a day visit in the abandoned part of Nessus, where he finds Dorcas sitting before the dead body of her husband, the old ferryman of the Garden of Endless Sleep who had been looking for "Cas." She had managed to return to him, but tragically too late—he has died. Severian slips away unseen.

Autarch: He also contains children (254).

Re-Echo: Phosphorescence and man-apes (256). This case is re-echo of a casting forward (II, chap. 6, 49).

Echo: Metaphor about dead city of Nessus (257) links to stone town rebuilding (II, chap. 31).

Curious Detail: "[A] little boat, newly built" (258).

Language of Flowers: Wilted scarlet poppy (258) means "fantastic extravagance," perhaps related to the boat; arum (260) means "ardor"; fern (260) means "fascination"; ivy means "matrimony, marriage, fidelity."

33. The Citadel of the Autarch

At the citadel Severian proves he is the new Autarch.

Echo: The ship's figurehead as anpiel (263) links to the anpiels at the war front (IV, chap. 20, 163), and before that to Severian's thoughts on the Gabriel story in the brown book (I, chap. 18, 162); the rowing song (264) links to the first day of his exile (I, chap. 14, 131).

Arthur Conan Doyle: The castellan is like Sherlock Holmes meeting Watson for the first time in *A Study in Scarlet* (1887), where first he says, "You have been in Afghanistan, I perceive," and later explains the chain of thought which had led him to this conclusion:

"'Here is a gentleman of a medical type, but with the air of a military man. Clearly an army doctor, then. He has just come from the tropics, for his face is dark, and that is not the natural tint of his skin, for his wrists are fair. He has undergone hardship and sickness, as his haggard face says clearly. His left arm has been injured. He holds it in a stiff and unnatural manner. Where in the tropics could an English army doctor have seen much hardship and got his arm wounded? Clearly in Afghanistan.'"

Compare this with Wolfe:

"But you have seen fighting, and you have been in the jungle north of the mountains, where no battle has been since they turned our flank by crossing the Uroboros."

"That's true," I said. "But how can you know?"

"That wound in your thigh came from one of their spears. I've seen enough to recognize them. . . . Not a cataphract, or they wouldn't have got you so easily. The demilances?"

"Only the light irregulars."

"You'll have to tell me about that later, because you're a city man from your accent, and they're ecclectics . . . You have a double scar on your foot too, white and clean with the marks half a span apart. That was a blood bat's bite, and they don't come that large except in the true jungle at the waist of the world" (265-66).

Robert Graves: Severian's claiming of the throne is satisfying, in contrast to that of Claudius's in *I, Claudius,* where the poor man is forced into it by soldiers after the assassination of the notorious Emperor Caligula in AD 41. In this manner Severian has a heroic validation compared with the farcical selection of Claudius, thus closing out the *I, Claudius* thread, even while Severian tells the reader that with this episode "we are come to the interval of comedy" (264).

34. The Key to the Universe

Severian tells the details of his talk with Master Palaemon.
    Echo: Fall into sky again (275) links to that night above Thrax (III, chap. 13, 100).
    Non-Linear Moment: What aquastor Malrubius told Severian (IV, chap. 31, 250) is finally revealed (IV, chap. 34, 278).

35. Father Inire's Letter

Severian receives a report from Father Inire.
    Apollo: The mandragora as sibyl (282). Recall that when the lusty wolf god attempted to seduce the Sibyl of Cumae, offering her as many years of life as she could grasp grains of sand, she forgot to ask for eternal youth, and became gray and decrepit, recognized only by her voice. This was told in Ovid's *Metamorphoses* (Book 14, Fable 3). Then there is Petronius's *The Satyricon,* in which Trimalchio says, "And then, there's the Sibyl: with my own eyes I saw her at Cumae, hanging up in a jar; and whenever the boys would say to her, 'Sibyl, Sibyl, what would you?' she would answer, 'I would die.'" (*The Satyricon,* chap. 48). This passage was later used as an epigraph to T. S. Eliot's poem "The Waste Land" (1922).
    Putting Names to Strange Allies at the Front: Inire's letter names the three groups at the Third Battle of Orithyia as the Tarantines, your Antrustions, and the city legions (288). Since the city legions were the "normal" forces, the unusual allies were presumably Antrustions (foreigners) and Tarantines (from the Greek colony of Tarantium). The two groups were the savage riders with their shaggy infantry, and the Daughters of War with their light cavalry. Tarantium was the only colony of Sparta, and this seems a key to seeing the infantry as helots, which might be why they are depicted as bestial yet are never called "man beasts." The Daughters of War seem to be the legendary Amazons translated into Persians, and they must be the Antrustions.

36. Of Bad Gold and Burning

Severian retrieves the hidden coin that Vodalus had given him that night in the graveyard—and in the frame tale, ten years later, he discovers that it was a counterfeit all along.

Mausoleum Detail: Door three-quarters shut (290).

Frame Tale Time: A few days ago, here to the House Absolute (291).

Commentary: Talos asks if Severian has a "slow explosive" so he can "blow people apart slowly" (293), which might describe Wolfe's slow reveal, for example, the Triskele miracle that is revealed over four volumes.

37. Across the River Again

Severian returns to the Inn of Lost Loves, interrogates Ouen the waiter as to the intrigue with the staff on his last visit, and determines not only that Ouen is the middle-aged son of Dorcas (who died in childbirth), but that Ouen is Severian's father, and Severian's mother is a former monial named Catherine. Severian takes Ouen to the dead city and commands him as Autarch to tell his life story to Dorcas, and to protect her with the laser pistol Severian gives him.

Rose: Death roses of the necropolis (298).

Echo: The old moonraker says, "There was things in the river up till first light" (299), which echoes Severian's first night out, when the lochage told him, "There's been some kind of trouble on the river, and they're telling each other too many ghost stories out there already" (I, chap. 14, 134).

A Thought for the Murder Victim: "[E]ven that ignorant and innocent man I killed with his own ax" (302) links to the opening chapter (I, chap. 1, 16).

Catherine: "She'd run off from some order of monials. The law got her, and I never saw her again" (306). That must have happened something like twenty-three years before. "Monials" evoke Pelerines, but "Catherine" implies Holy Katharine, patron of the torturers.

Commentary: The "little sister" turns out to be a grandmother, due to a form of time-travel. It seems likely that Catherine is also a time-traveler, being the woman at the torturers' feast every year, and presumably traveling back in time to become the "original" Katharine.

Then there is the mystery of the galleass and the smaller boat with big pale men (299-302) and an undine, where the galleass seems like Naviscaput.

38. Resurrection

Severian returns to the citadel and retraces his steps through the deep tunnels until he finds the Atrium of Time and calls out for Valeria.

The First Severian: "I am not the first Severian" (310). Severian guesses the following points about the life of the first Severian:

> He too was reared by the torturers, I think. He too was sent forth to Thrax. He too fled Thrax, and though he did not carry the Claw of the Conciliator, he must have been drawn to the fighting in the north—no doubt he hoped to escape the archon by hiding himself among the army. How he encountered the Autarch there I cannot say; but encounter him he did, and so, even as I, he (who in the final sense was and is myself) became Autarch in turn and sailed beyond the candles of night. Then those who walk the corridors walked back to the time when he was young, and my own story—as I have given it here in so many pages—began.
>
> The second thing is this. He was not returned to his own time but became himself a walker of the corridors. I know now the identity of the man called the Head of Day, and why Hildegrin, who was too near, perished when we met, and why the witches fled. I know too in whose mausoleum I tarried as a child, that little building of stone with its rose, its fountain, and its flying ship all graven. I have disturbed my own tomb, and now I go to lie in it. (310)

So the first Severian did the job without the childhood inspiration of the mausoleum, without the appearance of Apu-Punchau, and without the ambiguous aid of the Claw. To help Severian, the first Severian therefore built the mausoleum, arranged for Severian to obtain the Claw, and finally helped Severian by sacrificially besting Hildegrin in combat.

Triskele: Resurrected two years before I bore the Claw (311).

Echo: In the tunnels again, Severian sees ancient writing that reminds him of "the scrawlings of the rats" (312) in the Library (I, chap. 6).

Dickens: When Severian calls for Valeria (313), this closes the *Great Expectations* thread with a happier ending for Severian than either of the two endings (original and revised) for Pip.

Appendix: The Arms of the Autarch and the Ships of the Hierodules.

Wolfe traces three tiers of technology: smith level (metal melee weapons), Urth level (pyrotechnic polearms), and stellar level (energy rifles, and presumably energy pistols).

POSTLUDES FOR THE BOOK OF THE NEW SUN

Book Postlude 1: The First Severian

Near the end of his narrative, Severian drops a bombshell with: "I am not the first Severian" (IV, chap. 38, 310). He goes on to guess the following points about the life of the first Severian:

- He was raised by the torturers.
- He was sent to Thrax.
- He fled Thrax.
- Though he did not carry the Claw, he went north.
- He encountered the Autarch in the north and became Autarch himself.
- After his voyage to bring a New Sun, "he was not returned to his own time but became himself a walker of the corridors," becoming the vivimancer Apu-Punchau as well as the man who built the mausoleum in the necropolis.

Severian's working theory seems to be that his personal endpoint is the Apu-Punchau implosion, so that the mausoleum-building earlier in the posthistory must happen before he takes up vivimancy in the depths of prehistory.

Another way of putting this is that Severian knows his life is being rewritten by the meddling of time travelers who are clustered in at least three groups: one containing the three hierodules Ossipago, Barbatus, and Famulimus in their saucer-ship; another being the aquastors of Malrubius and Triskele in the second timeship; and finally the first Severian, who is perpetually in the personal future of Severian.

Considering each group in turn:

The saucer-fliers have trained Baldanders, who is an enemy of the New Sun, but they began their Urth-visit with years at Severian's court. While this seems to make their loyalty ambiguous, Severian never doubts Ossipago, Barbatus, and Famulimus. Their main meddling seems to be their boosting of Baldanders's science and the single encounter they have with Severian.

The second timeship, seemingly disguised as a watercraft common to the River Gyoll, is apparently the source for all the Malrubius and Triskele aquastors: at the near-drowning (I, chap. 2); on the day of Severian's elevation (I, chap. 11); at Ctesiphon's Cross (I, chap. 33); during fever in the lazaret (IV, chap. 4); and during the escape in the second timeship (IV, chap. 30 and chap. 34). Its range at projecting these phantoms "is but a few thousand years" (IV, chap. 31, 251), so it has probably returned to its home port that many years in the past. This faction communicates at least five times with Severian in the form of visions.

The first Severian plays two roles: mausoleum builder during the time of autarchs and Apu-Punchau in the far distant past. The mausoleum builder affects Severian through static objects like the symbols of the armorial device (fountain, flying ship, and rose) and the funereal bronze. Apu-Punchau encounters Severian the one time in the stone town. The first Severian probably controls the second timeship.

With all this manipulation by time travelers in mind, consider again the scene where Severian tracks Dorcas to her old home (IV, chap. 32): He sees the "little boat, newly built, tied to an ancient pier" (258) with "a wilted scarlet poppy left lying on the single seat" (258). He has the *Samru* drop him off and he tracks Dorcas in the dead city (258), perhaps by following the scent of her arum flower (259).

He walks a league or less, seeing no humans (259) in the notoriously savage wildlands. He comes upon her kneeling at the bier of her husband (260), where she had just arrived (261). This timing is crucial.

He leaves her and walks on to meet the *Samru*, where they think it a miracle to see him again.

It does seem incredible that neither Severian with his big borrowed craquemarte sword (258), nor little Dorcas with her picnic basket and water jar (260), encounters any trouble.

While the episode might seem so contrived as to make Charles Dickens blush, Dickens was never writing about time travelers. Who put the old man's body on the bier? For that matter, who sold Dorcas the boat? Who is keeping the scavengers at bay? Which is to say, who is "stage managing" this miracle? The mausoleum builder, of course!

Severian's statement about the first Severian encourages or demands speculation on how his narrative would be different if he had not possessed the Claw of the Conciliator.

Without the Claw, Severian would not meet Dorcas. Dorcas is a guard against Agia, but even more so the presence of the sword and the gem tempt Agia to try murder: without these complications of little sister, sword, and jewel, Agia might plausibly get along well with a simple adventurer Severian on his way to Thrax. But instead the crisis comes, Agilus loses his head, and Agia becomes Severian's sworn enemy.

The Claw also ruins the relationship between Severian and Baldanders, along the lines of "superstition versus science." Following this thought, it is possible that the Claw causes the fight to come sooner, as in the hypothetical case with Agia.

This "first Severian" angle gives a powerful rationale for the paradox of the vision dream, in allowing that each part was true for the first Severian, but not entirely true for the rewritten Severian. The first Severian rode the flying mount, dove into the sea, and was entertained by the undines who showed him a puppet play based upon a fight in his past; the second Severian was carried by the flying mount, but never swam with the undines nor saw the puppet play.

If the "dream" of Severian riding the flying monster was a vision of the experience of the first Severian, it might suggest that the first Severian and Agia were allies at that point when he set out to visit the undines, and furthermore that the first Severian had already had the break with Baldanders, which is why the undines showed the toy theatre battle (they were showing they knew it had happened, rather than showing a future event).

So perhaps the first Severian was friends with Baldanders, Agia, and Hethor (source of the flying mounts), but in the end each betrayed him at different points. The goal of the rewriting, then, would not be to remove these false friends from Severian's life, but to expose their flaws more rapidly, by someone who knows exactly what those flaws are: the first Severian.

The discrepancies between the vision dream and the later reality might also point to resolving the various "Paradoxes to Perfect Memory" scattered throughout the text. With all these time travelers meddling, the reality is changing even while Severian is writing. So it is true when he writes it was Roche who said the men had pikes, and a minute later it is true when he writes it was Drotte who said it. When he writes the little sack containing the Claw is made of doeskin it is true, just as when he writes it is made of manskin.

To summarize it, Severian sees the path ahead, blazed by the first Severian, as a sequence of three labors: first he will bring the New Sun; then he will go back in time to make the mausoleum; then he will go further back in time to be Apu-Punchau.

Book Postlude 2: Severian and Apollo

It stands to reason that if one wants to solve a dying sun scenario, one might craft a solar hero along the lines of a solar god like Apollo. Apollo turns out to be rather complex, a god of wolves, disease, seduction, and healing, as well as archery, music, poetry, prophecy, the Sun, light, and more.

Severian's meditations on the three Adonai (that of the city, the poets, and the philosophers) ends with the notion that they all lead in different directions. Yet the three Adonai can also be arranged as a sequence: Apollo as a child is a killer, as a youth he is a seducer, and as an adult he is a healer. Likewise, Severian as a boy is a murderer, as a youth he is a seducer, and as an adult he is a healer.

Apollo was not raised by his mother, but nursed by nymphs Korythalia and Aletheia. Since nymphs are aquatic, perhaps the undine who raised Severian from the water counts. Thecla certainly counts for the education she gave him, and since she wears a kraken bracelet (I, chap. 8), she is definitely a nymph.

Apollo has a twin, and Severian has a twin. Both Apollo and Severian are linked to wolves.

Apollo received the triskele as a child. Severian revived a three-legged dog named Triskele.

Hera was the enemy of child Apollo, and her symbol is the peacock. Soon after leaving his home, Severian became a target of Agia, who wore a peacock dress.

Apollo killed Python, nurse of Typhon; Severian killed Piaton, whose body had been usurped by Monarch Typhon.

Apollo became a healer somehow; Severian struggles to control the miraculous healing of the Claw of the Conciliator. Apollo was a god of disease, and Severian seems to have conquered a disease in his healing of the dead soldier.

Apollo had to go up to Mount Olympus, the realm of the gods, to make his place among them. Severian must go to Yesod, the higher universe, to plead for a new sun.

Book Postlude 3: Resurrect Only What You Kill

On the darker side, Severian seems to have a nebulous notion that he can only resurrect a creature he has himself killed, a logic that might spring from the mindset of a stone age hunter, where totem animals are brought back to life by the hunter-magician in sacred rituals.

Throughout his narrative Severian stumbles through the murky maze of his own powers, trying to grasp the rules of healing and resurrection. He struggles to understand why the Claw of the Conciliator works miracles on some occasions and fails to work at others. At one point fairly late in the game, he tells "Miles," the dead soldier he had just resurrected:

> "It cured the man-ape whose hand I had cut away. Perhaps that was because I had done it myself. And it helped Jonas, but I—Thecla— had used those whips." (IV, chap. 3, 28)

On the surface this seems immediately wrong as a working theory. Yes, it works for the man-ape, and for Thecla herself (since Severian gave her the knife which she used for suicide); it also works for the uhlan resurrected at the House Absolute (Severian had prayed that the notules would kill the soldier rather than him). As he has killed them, so he has raised them up again.

But the model breaks down in two early cases of unambiguous resurrection, those of Dorcas the girl and Triskele the dog. After all, how could Severian be responsible for the death of his grandmother Dorcas, an event that happened decades before his own birth? And Triskele the mastiff was killed in blood sport with other animals, so how could there be a connection with Severian? A working theory that cannot address these two cases would seem to be fatally flawed.

However that may be, it is wrong to discount Severian's notion so quickly and easily, since later in the text we get more details about Triskele's demise:

> There was an arsinoither and a smilodon, and several dire wolves. The dog was lying on top. I suppose he had been the last to die, and from his wounds one of the dire wolves had killed him. (IV, chap. 18, p. 141)

So here, in this third version of the discovery of Triskele (the first being at I, chap. 4, 37; the second being at III, chap. 20, 161), we learn at last that a wolf killed the dog. Add to this the thin but sure thread that Severian is a wolf, and presto! It is clear and plain that Severian was able to raise Triskele because Severian killed him.

Then there is Dorcas. If we accept Ouen's word that she died in childbirth, then it is a short step to posit that the child who "killed" her was Ouen. The trail of generational guilt, from father Ouen to son Severian, is certainly easier to track than the wispy wolf trail.

The "working theory" gains considerable heft.

•

The Cases of Resurrection
1) Dorcas—killed by childbirth (Ouen), spontaneously resurrected by the hidden Claw.
2) Thecla—suicide by Severian's help (knife), resurrected within Severian.
3) The uhlan—killed by Severian's bargain (notule), resurrected with the Claw.
4) Typhon—dead for chiliads, spontaneously resurrected by the Claw.
5) Miles resurrected/Jonas's soul invades—Jonas's suicide by Severian's help (mirror).
6) Triskele—killed by a dire wolf, resurrected by Severian alone.

In five out of six cases the text is clear that Severian is responsible, even if only through proxy of blood relative (Ouen) or a wolf. The situation with Typhon is a puzzler, unless it goes backwards, since Severian later kills Typhon.

The pattern also shows up in Severian's attempts at mere healing. As mentioned in the quote before, Severian cured the man-ape near Saltus and Jonas in the antechamber, both of whom he had wounded (one directly and the other by way of Thecla's behavior in the past). But then there are his failures with the Claw, which include his attempts to heal Jolenta (II, chap. 28, 263) and his try at healing all the patients in the lazaret field hospital (IV, chap. 8, 66). For Jolenta it seems that she is doomed because her condition is not Severian's fault. With the patients in the lazaret it seems perhaps more a power limitation: Severian is still learning and his power allowance is not enough for a group healing; yet as a proof of concept exercise, the light of the Claw does do some restorative good to the prisoners of Thrax (III, chap. 12, 97).

The healing of the children in the jacal of Thrax (III, chap. 8) is ambiguous. The text at first suggests it is "paid for" by Severian's killing of Cyriaca, but when this fake out is revealed there is not anything left to go on. It might be the first hint of Severian's "god of disease" aspect, which later shows up with the dead soldier.

The healing of the young outlaw Manahan (II, chap. 29) might be another "it goes backwards" example, since Severian subsequently wounds Manahan's father.

Severian's various failures with the Claw do not lead him to abandon attempts at healing, but there is a lingering suspicion that he can only resurrect those he has killed.

Book Postlude 4: Conan the Proustian

What follows is sympathy for those readers who find Severian to be the opposite of what they look for in a genre hero.

The tetralogy opens with a solid hook: the kid gets drawn into the rebellion and kills a man, his "first blood" initiation.

But then . . . nothing happens. Severian is passive, more acted upon than acting. Part of this is baked in with the bildungsroman format, since characters growing from childhood into adulthood are being shaped and formed by guardians and society.

For contrast consider Robert E. Howard's Conan the Cimmerian, in many ways the model of the modern genre hero. Not only is Conan a man of manly action, but when he is introduced in the first story "The Phoenix and the Sword" (1932) he is already the king of a civilized country, a man who has somehow or another clawed his way up to that station from being a barbarian outsider, surprisingly similar to Severian's situation. Most of the subsequent Conan stories are about a younger hero, beginning with "The Tower of the Elephant" (1933). This shows by example that every episode in a hero's life can be an action adventure, even when it is known that he will eventually become a king.

When Severian leaves the citadel of his upbringing there is the potential that he will be able to act on his own. This bears some fruit at the bridge when the commander tells him to prove his training, and Severian uses an exotic technique. But shortly thereafter he is being manipulated by Agia and Agilus. The avern duel, the volume's big event, is outside Severian's training and is rapidly finished. The execution of Agilus is within his training but by no means is it heroic.

The mine at Saltus provides a good romp, and the pursuit by notules is a gripping flight, but these bursts of action are few and far between. *The Sword of the Lictor* is the most action-packed volume, from the salamander scrimmage in chapter 9 to the battle with Baldanders in chapter 35, yet the solutions are not heroic: the contest with the salamander is won by dumb luck; the final fight with the alzabo is disastrous; the sorcery duel is won by the intrusion of a wandering monster; the trial with Typhon is clinched with a trick; and the fight with the giant leads to the loss of both the magic sword and the sacred gem. Never mind "not heroic": these victories are pyrrhic.

There is even a moment when Agilus calls Severian an uncivilized outsider: "Agia and I wore the gaudy armor of a barbarian—you wore his heart" (I, chap. 29, 253). For genre readers this is close to calling Severian "Conan," especially since both end up on their respective thrones.

Yet Severian has that Proustian process, a way of meditative meandering that gives many of the most memorable lines. For example, the paragraph beginning, "We believe that we invent symbols. The truth is that they invent us; we are their creatures, shaped by their hard, defining edges" (I, chap. 1, 17). Then there is a favorite of Neil Gaiman and many others: "We are like children who look at print and see a serpent in the last letter but one, and a sword in the last" (III, chap. 30, 241).

INTERLUDE: THE SHORTER WORKS OF THE NEW SUN

- "The God and His Man" (collected in *Endangered Species)*
- *Empires of Foliage and Flower* (collected in *Starwater Strains)*
- "The Cat" (collected in *Endangered Species)*
- "The Map" (collected in *Endangered Species)*

"The God and His Man" (collected in *Endangered Species*)

A sentient starship "god" summons a man from Urth to survey the planet Zed on foot. The god gives Man a cloak of invisibility and a magic sword to aid him in this.

Man starts in the desert where men have few laws and many slaves. After learning his way around, Man becomes a warlord and builds a citadel in the mountains. Growing tired of this, he goes into the jungle.

In the jungle Man learns a new way, taming a panther and becoming the leader of a new religion. He enjoys the pleasures of this place until the god prods him to move on.

So Man goes to the cold lands, where the people have many laws but no slaves. After a while he becomes a wandering philosopher.

But then the god calls him up to report, asking which of the three peoples he loves the best.

Man says the jungle people, because they fall between the injustice of the desert and the justice of the cold lands.

The god criticizes him, saying the people of the cold lands are nearest to him. He says that the jungle, and then the world, will be conquered by either the desert people or the cold lands people. He then shows the cold people colonizing the jungle and driving its people into enclosed areas "where they sat in the dust until they died" (*Endangered Species*, 208).

Man points out that the unjust desert people make slaves of the jungle people, but the slaves still live.

The god says, "It is better that a man should die than that he should be a slave."

Man kills the god with the sword.

Jack Vance: This tale is like two stories in *The Dying Earth*. The beginning is like the middle of "Turjan of Miir," where the hero is tasked with a quest by a superior sorcerer. The ending is like the climax of "Ulan Dhor," where the hero uses his sword against the insane god. "Ulan Dhor" links to "The

Cleansing" (II, chap. 31). "Turjan of Miir" links to "Agilus," (I, chap. 29), "The Tale of the Student and His Son" (II, chap. 17), and "Cyriaca" (III, chap. 5).

Lord Dunsany: The story has a certain whimsy, as seen where the god's name is "Isid Iooo IoooE" (*Endangered Species*, 203); and there are British terms "Zed" (203) and "spinney" (206).

German: The cloak is named "Tarnung" (204), German for cloak or camouflage.

Americana: "Maser," the magic sword, is named after a device invented in the US in 1953.

Arabian Nights: The citadel of roses in the mountains sounds like the fortress of the Assassins.

Kipling: The steaming lands seem a bit Jungle Book with Mowgli and his friend Bagheera the black panther. Mowgli and Bagheera link to "The Tale of the Boy Called Frog" (III, chap. 19).

Bible: The line "He let Man see through his own eyes" (204) is a strong link to Typhon's temptation of Severian in "The Eyes of the World" (III, chap. 26), which draws from the Temptation of Jesus (Matthew 4: 8-9).

History of Science: "Then while Man watched through his eyes, certain good men in the cold lands died, which men called lightning. Certain evil men died also, and men spoke of disease" (208). These two sentences seem to obliquely say that science advances through deadly experimentation that kills good men (scientists, for example) and evil men (convicts who volunteer as guinea pigs, perhaps).

In the story, after the conquest of "lightning" and "disease," the people of the cold lands colonize the steaming lands. In our world the European colonization of the tropics was made possible by discoveries in electricity and medicine. Perhaps the story is addressing the invention of electrical air conditioning (USA, 1902) and tropical medicine (UK, 1899).

Commentary: The scenario is that the steaming lands will be overrun by people from either the high, hot lands or the cold lands. Presumably this will only happen through influence from the god: the question is which one will be the invaders, and the god has already decided on that, too. The dilemma is that the hot lands people will use slavery, whereas the cold lands people will use passive genocide.

The god is claimed to be "good" (203), yet when given the choice between slavery or genocide, he goes with genocide. To the man, genocide is obviously not good, being worse than slavery. He kills the god as a false god. Since the man wanted the status quo, this is also a win on that front.

Empires of Foliage and Flower (collected in *Starwater Strains)*

This tale is summarized in *The Book of the New Sun* through a conversation between the Cumaean and Severian:

> "In ancient days, in a land far off, there stood two empires, divided by mountains. One dressed its soldiers in yellow, the other in green. For a hundred generations they struggled. I see that the man with you knows the tale."
> "And after a hundred generations," I said, "an eremite came along them and counseled the emperor of the yellow army to dress his men in green, and the master of the green army that he should clothe it in yellow. But the battle continued as before. In my sabretache, I have a book called *The Wonders of Urth and Sky,* and the story is told there." (III, chap. 31, 289)

Here is a more expansive synopsis: Father Thyme is the eremite, a sage who ages as he walks west and grows young as he walks east. He finds a young child playing at war and peace with some peas in the dust and takes her on a quest to end the conflict between the two empires. The child ages as she travels with Thyme, such that she is seduced as a young woman by the green Prince Patizithes; gives birth to a son in the mountains the next day; and enters the yellow capital as an old woman with a teenage son. Barrus, the son, is taken hostage by the Yellow Emperor, and Thyme takes the child back east, where the green capital now seems to be under new management. Thyme leaves the child at the yard where he had found her, an infant again.

Lord Dunsany: The whimsical logic of herbal eremites; the pattern of alliteration.

Language of Flowers: There are a bunch frontloaded (*Starwater Strains,* 246). Sage is "Esteem." Acacia is "Friendship." Fennel is "Worthy of all praise; Strength." Orchis is "A Belle." Basil is "Hatred." Lichen is

"Dejection." Eglantine is "Poetry; I wound to heal." Thyme is "Activity."

Persian: The green prince Patizithes has a Persian name.

Technology: The term "grenadiers" (258) suggests a 17th century soldier type that seems more advanced than the medieval/renaissance types listed throughout Severian's narrative.

Wolf: Wolves howling at the battlefield (258).

Horace: The name Barrus seems a Latin name, at least through the association made by the yellow soldier, who says, "The handsome one, eh?" (259). The Roman poet Horace (65-8 BC) in "Satire #6" wrote about a vain contemporary, "It's as if you had Barrus's disease, Who wished to be thought of as handsome."

Follower of the Conciliator: The yellow soldier seems to be a follower of the Conciliator. He says "By the book!" and "What in the name of awful Abaia are you two up to?" (259). More importantly, he sees her need and gives her his gray cloak (260).

This sacrifice moves her profoundly, and later she tells Thyme "those who have seen clean water in the desert's depths, without drinking, are entitled to tears" (260), which builds on the previous metaphor about love, where she had asked him, "Wouldn't it be better not to know love at all, than to know a false love?" To which he said, "In the desert, travelers see pools of water where no water is; but those who see these pools know how real water must look, if ever real water is found" (258). Thus, she recognizes a true love in the soldier's sacrifice to her.

Bible: "Naked, and ye clothed me" (Matthew 25:36); "Inasmuch as ye have done it unto one of the least of these my brethren, ye have done it unto me" (Matthew 25:40).

"And if any man will sue thee at the law, and take away thy coat, let him have they cloak also" (Matthew 5:40).

"Give to every man that asketh of thee; and of him that taketh away thy goods ask them not again" (Luke 6:30).

Time Warpage: The story presents a lot of time-bending on the surface, in the way that Thyme and the child grow older and younger in their travels, and wine turns sour in Thyme's hands, et cetera. But below the surface it seems that time warping goes "both" ways, subjective and objective. That is, they seem to have been walking back and forth in time. The mountain pass on their return has skeletons covered with plants (270), suggesting a long passage of time since their visit before. Yes, these bones could be from previous warfare, but other details come when they return to Vert, now guarded by silver-clad soldiers beneath a silver flag (271), so it seems they have returned to an altered present. And when the child is reunited with her mother (271), it seems the baby had been missing for hours rather than the subjective six days of her adventure.

So they have walked back in time enough that both empires switch their colors and meet for a final battle; the Yellow Empire wins; and Barrus, having proven himself a faithful vassal (269), is installed on the throne of now-silver Vert.

We might base a guess on how deep in the past they have traveled by how old the child gets. In Xanth she is "A worn old woman" (265), so perhaps as much as fifty years.

Patizithes is a historical figure of ancient Persia, a man who tried a clever strategy of camouflage but was found out and his side lost. This matches the role Prince Patizithes plays in *Empires of Foliage and Flower*.

The time-warpage outlined here makes imaginable an Oedipal situation wherein a thirty-year-old son (Barrus) kills his twenty-year-old father (Patizithes), while his mother is an infant.

"The Cat" (collected in *Endangered Species*)

A story written down in the fifth year of Severian's reign, about strange events and court intrigue in the House Absolute in a previous generation. In brief, a seven-year-old exultant child named Sancha threw her cat into Father Inire's magic mirrors, and it was scattered. Thereafter she had a sort of phantom cat. At age fourteen Sancha was tarnished in a scandal engineered by Chatelaine Leocadia to embarrass another chatelaine. At age twenty-one Sancha moved away, married, and raised a family. Fifty years later she returned to the House Absolute as a widow. When she died of old age, a pawprint appeared on the counterpane of her deathbed, along with a curious little doll creature now dead. Yet after Sancha's death, Leocadia has been haunted by a phantom cat.

Commentary: Sancha's cat was brought back by Inire as a kind of familiar. Sancha did not want to be a witch, yet she had this familiar, and people began to talk. As a teen Sancha was stained by the Leocadia-crafted scandal, yet Leocadia "suffered nothing" at that time (215). Sancha went away and raised a family, yet when she returned in her old age she complained that her daughter-in-law had called her a witch (216). Her whole life from age seven had been shadowed by this witchy reputation, yet she had never done anything to deserve it. When she died, then something started happening.

I think that the familiar was a ghost cat bound to that little flesh doll, a creature that was invisible until it died. I think the flesh doll looked like a little girl because Sancha was the cat's goddess and what the cat wanted to be; but the cat was still a cat and behaved like a cat. I think Sancha kept a tight rein on her familiar, but it still managed catlike mischief. When Sancha died, the familiar lost its doll anchor and also lost any controlling force, so it set out on revenge, and Leocadia began to suffer.

"The Map" (collected in *Endangered Species)*

In this story set during Severian's reign, the former torturer's apprentice Eata wakes up on his boat having gained a headwound and lost some property, both due to former friends Syntyche and Laetus betraying him. A bookish adventurer calling himself Simulatio hires Eata for passage downriver to the dead city of Nessus. During the night on the river they encounter the murdered body of Syntyche. The next day Simulatio goes alone into the ruins, trying to follow his secret treasure map, but he is saved from death at the last minute by Eata. Eata takes wounded Simulatio back up the river to an inn, and admits that a similar map caused him his recent trouble, and likely trouble before that.

Unusual Spelling: The story uses "warf" instead of "wharf." The *Oxford English Dictionary* tells that "warf" is an obsolete form of "wharf."

Echoes: Eata is a character from the opening chapters of volume I. He also appears near the end of volume IV, when he first meets Maxellindis and her uncle the old moonraker (IV, chap. 37, 289; 307).

But there is also a curious echo in Simulatio's thoughts on the towers leaping into the sky: "You can almost imagine them going up, can't you?" he said. "Just taking off with a silver shout and leaving this world behind . . . . That's what they're supposed to do, at the end of time. I read about it somewhere" (24). It implies that he has read Severian's narrative or another text that Severian had imitated, as Severian wrote: "[I]ts thousand metal towers ready to leap into the air at a word" (IV, chap. 37, 302).

There is also the similarity of the glowing bits. For Simulatio on the river at night among the ruins, "Its towers were black, but their sightless windows, thus illuminated from behind, appeared to betray a faint radiance, as though hecatonchires roved the gloomy corridors and deserted rooms, their thousand fingers smeared with noctoluscence to light their way" (26). Severian wrote "On one such night, shortly after we had passed through the Wall, I went aft and saw the phosphorescence of our wake like cold fire . . .

and thought for a moment that the man-apes of the mine were coming" (IV, chap. 32, 256); an illusion that was so striking he had mentioned it in an earlier volume (II, chap. 6, 49).

Commentary: "The Map" makes good on the promise of dangerous adventure in the dead city in a way that was not possible in Severian's narrative. This gives a view of what it is like for most people.

Simulatio is a bookish adventurer, a semi-Severian, but through other echoes he might be Cyriaca's cousin: recall that the armigette's uncle was a book hunter who had visited the Library of Nessus, a detail forming the framing for her tale to Severian. Simulatio found his map between the pages of an old book (34).

Eata's comment "I knew a man who had one of those maps. A man can spend half his life looking, and never find a thing" (34) suggests that Eata's map had come from the old moonraker, Maxellindis's uncle. It was the moonraker who had wasted half his life searching. This notion of the map's provenance is furthered when Eata says he had wasted Maxellindis's life searching for the treasure (34).

POSTLUDE FOR THE SHORTER
WORKS OF THE NEW SUN

Two Brown Books (the One and the Other)

In Severian's narrative there is a special place for *The Book of the Wonders of Urth and Sky,* known familiarly as "the brown book." Outside of Severian's narrative there are stories that may or may not be tales from the brown book. *Empires of Foliage and Flower* is definitely from the brown book, since it is referred to as such within Severian's narrative. "The God and His Man" might be in the brown book, but "The Cat" and "The Map" are definitely not, being stories set on Urth.

Then there is "The Boy Who Hooked the Sun" (1985). It has the flavor of an Urth story, yet it seems in a gray area, even though it is subtitled "A Tale from The Book of the Wonders of Urth and Sky." In the Introduction to the collection *Starwater Strains,* Wolfe wrote "It's a brown book story, like those in "From the Cradle"" (16). That is interesting, because "From the Cradle" is set in a near future Earth, rather than Urth; the book therein is called "Browne's Book—Wonders of ~" (107). The stories within this story are "The Tale of the Dwarf and the Children of the Sphinx" (99); "The Tale of Prince Know-Nothing" (104); and "The Tale of the Boy and the Bookshop" (107). So it seems that there is this "other" brown book. Just as there are at least two works titled "The Book of the New Sun," the one written by Severian and the other being a holy text begun by Canog.

VOLUME V: THE URTH OF THE NEW SUN

Dedication: "This book is dedicated to Elliott and Barbara, who know why." Nigel Price tells me that the "Elliot and Barbara" in question are Mr. and Mrs. Swanson. Elliott Swanson interviewed Gene Wolfe for *Interzone* in 1986, a piece collected in Wright's *Shadows of the New Sun*. Elliott Swanson was also in the dedication to Wolfe's novel *Castleview* (1990). Nigel Price has yet to hear the backstory to the *Urth* dedication, but he persists.

> *Awake! for Morning in the Bowl of Night*
> *Has flung the Stone that puts the Stars to Flight:*
> *And Lo! the Hunter of the East has caught*
> *The Sultan's Turret in a Noose of Light*
> —Fitzgerald

Epigraph: Quote from Edward Fitzgerald, as cited in the text. This is the first stanza of "The Rubaiyat of Omar Khayyam" (1859). Note that the flinging of a stone into the cup was the signal "To horse!" in the desert.

1. The Mainmast

After reigning for ten years, Severian boards the starship of Tzadkiel for the journey to Yesod, the higher universe where he will plead for a new sun on behalf of Urth. He goes onto the deck to throw his manuscript overboard but ends up falling into space.

Epithets: The two epithets for Severian as "the Lame" and "the Great" (1) point to at least two historical figures. The Roman Emperor Claudius had a limp due to childhood illness, and Robert Graves's *I, Claudius* is an important model for Severian's narrative. On the darker side is an echo to Tamur the Lame, Tamur the Great. Marlowe's play "Tamburlaine the Great"

(1587); Poe's early poem "Tamerlane" (1827).

Frame Tale: Severian sets the time he is writing about as being "a few years ago" (1); at that time he wrote about a time around ten years past, but now that same period is a century or more in the past (2).

Poe: Severian plans "to wait until our vessel had penetrated the fabric of time" (6) before throwing his narrative into the void. This strategy is straight from Poe's story, "MS. Found in a Bottle" (1833), which describes a man on a haunted ship, heading into increasing strangeness. Poe's hero writes, "At the last moment I will enclose the MS. in a bottle, and cast it within the sea." His last report says, "[A]bout a league on either side of us . . . stupendous ramparts of ice, towering away into the desolate sky, and looking like the walls of the universe," and then he tosses his tale-bearing-bottle overboard as the vessel plunges toward a polar entrance to a hollow earth.

2. The Fifth Sailor

Severian manages to get back to the deck of the ship, but in a different section from where he had started. He meets middle-aged Burgundofara (she prefers "Gunnie"), Purn, and albino Idas, led by Sidero, an iron-class mechanical officer. They are hunting for "apports," escaped or newly arrived creatures running lose on the ship, and they press Severian into service. Then Sidero pushes him off a ledge.

Chapter Title Mystery: The fifth sailor is presumably Severian.

Memory Boast: For those keeping track (11).

Thematic Echo: Severian falls up (9), an unremarked link to his fears of falling up into the sky on his night above Thrax (III, chap. 13, 100).

3. The Cabin

After falling in the low gravity, Severian finds the shaggy apport and helps capture it, then he finds a new cabin for himself next to Gunnie's in the crew section.

Revenge: Severian wants revenge for Sidero's pushing him off the ledge (17).

Animal Form: Gunnie's cow eyes (18); Gunnie as large blue bird (20).

Adultery: Severian moves toward adultery (21-22).

4. The Citizens of the Sails

After wandering around in the surreal landscape of the ship, Severian finds his old stateroom again.

Echo: "[W]ith the aquastor Malrubius" (23) links to the "dissolve on the beach" scene (IV, chap. 31, 251).

Wolf: "[M]ore terrible than the howling of a dire-wolf" (24).

Echo: Quoting Hethor, "Long I signed . . ." (26), is from Severian's meeting of the old sailor at Ctesiphon's Cross (I, chap. 35, 291).

Big White Moon: Purn's question (27) suggests he comes from a time before the terraforming of Lune.

Thematic Echo: Idas telling about feeding the apports (28) recalls Hethor's rants on feeding creatures: "I the old captain, the old lieutenant, the old c-c-cook in his old kitchen, cooking soup, cooking broth for the dying pets!" (I, chap. 35, 292).

Memory Boast and Direction Failure: Severian acknowledges his previous failure to follow directions of the lochage on the bridge (28), linking to that scene (I, chap. 15, 136).

5. The Hero and the Hierodules

The hierodules Ossipago, Barbatus, and Famulimus visit Severian, meeting him for their "first time," and since they are moving backwards through time, he knows that this will be the last time he sees them. He visits their strange quarters.

Animal Form: Famulimus having the voice of a lark (32).

Myth: "Kelpies" (35) are lowland Scottish water-spirits that haunt lakes and rivers. Usually appearing as horses, they delight in the drowning of people.

6. A Death and the Dark

Outside the quarters of the hierodules Severian finds a murdered crewman, his steward. He tries to use the thorn-Claw to resurrect him but it does not work: instead the gangway is plunged into darkness and Severian feels very sick. He shoots his laser pistol on low setting and clips a would-be assailant. Severian searches through the dark ship for the seared killer and is jumped by someone else in the hold. The shaggy apport bites this attacker.

Animal: Blood bat comes up again (38).

Frame Tale: Mention of the sunken Commonwealth (42) is the first evidence of deluge.

7. A Death in the Light

The attacker escapes the hold and the lights come back on. Back in his crew cabin Severian finds Idas, the tall albino sailor. They end up fighting—it turns out Idas is actually an undine child sent to assassinate him, but she commits suicide before he can question her much.

Revenge: Severian intends to kill his would-be assassin if the authorities take no action (46).

Great Lords: When Idas mentions "Great Lords who dwell in the sea and underground" (52), we immediately think of the watery lords Abaia and Erebus, but this is the first hint of subterraneans. It forms a possible link to the giant creature below the Saltus Mine (II, chap. 6, 55), and a probable link to Arioch (IV, chap. 1, 9).

Mystery: Idas was looking for the letter, and she successfully destroyed it. But what was the other item that could be hidden in a seam (53) of clothing? She does not answer, but the thorn-Claw seems likely.

8. The Empty Sleeve

Severian wants to report the death of Idas to the mysterious captain whom he has never met, so he wanders through the ship again. He finds Sidero with one arm torn off and learns that there is a mutiny in progress.

Ten Chrisos: Idas's supply of ten gold coins (55) recalls a detail in the movie *From Russia with Love* (1963), where James Bond's attache case has a hidden cache of fifty gold sovereigns.

Only One Ship: Sidero tells Severian, "There is only one ship, the captain says" (59). This had come up before, when Purn said something similar (26).

Wolf: Wolves communicate (60).

9. The Empty Air

Severian climbs inside of Sidero, using him as a suit of armor, and fights a strange pale monster with large wings. He is thrown down an airshaft and has a vision of his own death. When he wakes up at the bottom of the airshaft, he is being helped by a hairy dwarf named Zak and later tended by Gunnie. There is no sign of Sidero.

Echo: The struggle against the monster (64) shows thematic echoes of identity confusion with the meeting of Hildegrin and Apu-Punchau (II, chap. 31, 294). Which leads into an echo of Thecla and the Revolutionary (I, chap. 12, 118).

Echo: Final lines from the character The Prophet (65) in the play, originally given as: "In future times, so it has long been said, the death of the old sun will destroy Urth. But from its grave will rise monsters, a new people, and the New Sun. Old Urth will flower as a butterfly from its dry husk, and the New Urth shall be called Ushas" (II, chap. 24, 223). Then the orbiting skulls (67) link to the ceremonial ritual (IV, chap. 28, 226).

Condition: Severian is missing teeth due to the beating he received (67).

10. Interlude

Following a few sleep periods and a romantic tryst, Severian tells Gunnie he knows that she was the assailant he clipped with the laser.

Robert A. Heinlein: Calling the jibers "muties" (74) forms a link to Heinlein's "Universe" (1941), where the mutineers are also mutants (one has a club foot; another has two heads).

Revenge: Severian figures Sidero beat him when he was unconscious and vows he will kill him for that (75).

Adultery: Attempt fails, as spirit is willing, but flesh is unable (75).

11. Skirmish

Later Severian and Zak fall in with some loyal sailors hunting "jibers" (mutineers). Purn is with them. Severian figures out that Purn was the assailant bitten by the apport—and that the apport had subsequently metamorphosed into Zak.

Robert A. Heinlein: The "indigo giant" (79) points to the "mutie" side; as does the one with "the teeth of an atrox" (80).

Sailor Talk: When the sailor says to Severian, "like the hog told the butcher" (81), he is identifying Severian as a butcher. This might be as mild as alluding to Severian's earlier occupation as a torturer, and Severian had once referred to himself as "a butcher of men" (III, chap. 14, 112), or it might be much worse.

12. The Semblance

Purn admits to being a sailor-assassin from the Commonwealth of Severian's era, sent to kill Severian to save Urth from the destruction that will happen if the New Sun comes. Purn escapes. Severian asks Zak if he is the apport and Zak runs away. Then Severian is captured and bound by jibers.

Bible: While "The kiss is the sign" (84) might mean something in sailor culture, Gunnie's kiss sounds ominously like the Judas-kiss.

Stark Reversal: The line "turn Urth upside down and kill everybody" (85) makes plain how very different the situation is from what Severian thought at the end of *The Citadel of the Autarch,* where his last line is: "To this account, I, Severian . . . do set my hand in what shall be called the last year of the old sun" (313). He clearly thought he would return from Yesod to a renewed, improved world, where the Commonwealth would enjoy the benefits of a new sun.

Echo: Recalling dream of little Severian (85).

Animal: Yellow beard snake as evil (86).

13. The Battles

There is a brief fight and Severian is rescued by Sidero. Among Sidero's band of loyalist sailors is a man who introduces himself as Zak, metamorphosed again. Sidero refuses to believe Severian is Autarch of Urth and assigns him to the rearguard. There is a big battle with jibers, and the hull is breached.

Animal: Bear versus wolf combat (91).

Isaac Asimov: Sidero says, "We [robots] may sacrifice men to save our own existence. We may transmit and originate instructions to men. We may correct and chastise. But we may not become as you are. That is what I did [in having joy at beating Severian]. I must repay" (94).

This contradicts every single one of Asimov's famous "Three Laws of Robotics," first introduced in the short story "Runaround" (1942):

1. A robot may not injure a human being or, through inaction, allow a human being to come to harm.
2. A robot must obey the orders given it by humans except when such orders would conflict with the First Law.
3. A robot must protect its own existence as long as such protection does not conflict with the First or Second Laws.

14. The End of the Universe

The battle moves to the forest of the masts, where jibers struggle to cut down sails. Severian fights with a humanoid who has the hands of an arctother. Severian wins and the ship leaves Briah (normal space), entering the hyperspace of Yesod.

Echo: The icy deck (98) links to the plain of ice seen from Master Ash's window (IV, chap. 17, 131); the Master Ash quote (99) links to the scene by the window (IV, chap. 17, 133).

Robert A. Heinlein: Mutie with bear claws (100-101).

Leagues, Non-Literal: "[T]he mighty Wall of Nessus, a few leagues in height and a few thousand long" (103). These units are poetic, surely. See also notes for "Into the Mountains" (III, chap. 13).

Echo: Allusion (104) links to when Severian first visited the Autarch's suite in the Great Keep (IV, chap. 35, 281). Allusion to the Claw (104) links to the moment when Severian had first drawn it forth (I, chap. 31, 268).

15. Yesod

The sails are immediately reefed. Severian looks for the flier that will take him to the surface of planet Yesod, but he falls in with a royal procession of sailors and officers following a tall, naked man with bound hands.

Echo: Memory of sudden terror (106) links to the attack of the notules (II, chap. 13, 104); another memory links to the first evening of his exile from the Old Citadel (I, chap. 14, 130).

Animal: Wolf (107); pard (108), being a leopard.

Echo: Night is coming in "The Tale of the Student and His Son" (107), a link to a scene in that story (II, chap 17, 151).

Gravity: "[O]nly the slight pull of the holds, as it had been in the void" (107). This is curious by itself, and it may be the solution to the mystery of varying weight (chap. 8, 56), with increased gravity being limited to the level of the holds.

Bible: The noble captive followed by three persons, a man and two women (110), seems like an allusion to Jesus on his way to the crucifixion being followed by John, Mary Magdalene, and the Virgin Mary.

16. The Epitome

The royal prisoner is as tall as an exultant, at least, and has golden hair. The crowd believes him to be the Autarch of Urth—Gunnie and Purn stop Severian from trying to convince them otherwise, telling him he is a trickster or delusional. On the flier Gunnie points out that since the ship of Tzadkiel sails back and forth through Time, the golden one could possibly be one of Severian's successors to the throne.

Echo: Association of surroundings (112) links to fair at Saltus (II, chap. 3); Severian stood, "trying to understand why it was so" (112), and one answer is that the fair was prelude to execution, but in the next paragraph Severian says it is the sound of air rushing by, mimicking the sound of the river by Saltus.

Animal: Teratornis (114), swallow.

Echo: Fear of pentadactyls (114) links to the eerie passage of the pentadactyls (IV, chap. 21, 166).

Gunnie: This being her second voyage to Yesod, she was probably on the ship when the old Autarch was on his trip (115).

Enigmatic Memory from a Distant Autarch:

A memory rose, sent by one of those dim figures who stand, for me, behind the old Autarch, those predecessors whom I cannot see clearly and often cannot see at all. It was the figure of a lovely virgin, clothed in silks of many hues and dewed with pearls. She sang in the avenues of Nessus and lingered by its fountains until night. No one dared to molest her, for though her protector was invisible, his shadow fell all around her, rendering her inviolate. (116-17)

This passage describes something hauntingly similar to Dorcas's adventure in the dead city of Nessus (IV, chap. 32, 258-61), where it seems that both she and Severian are under the Aegis of some higher power, a protection from the danger of the place. As such, this might be an echo/presentiment of the impulse directing the first Severian to manage that scene in such a fashion. (See also "Book Postlude 1: The First Severian.")

17. The Isle

The party is dropped off on an isle. Severian meets Apheta, the middle-aged woman who had spoken to the crowd before. From her he learns that the golden one will be judged by the Hierogrammate Tzadkiel the next day, and that Severian will now lead him into the courtroom. As he does so, he calls the golden one "Zak," recognizing that the apport has metamorphosed again. Zak flees down the corridor.

First Impressions: Severian's first sight of Apheta compared with his first sight of Agia (120) further acknowledges Agia's deep impact upon him.

Echo: Allusion to youthful vigor (123) links to his first day of exile (I, chap. 14, 130). Series of pictures (123): a wide, empty hall lined with mirrors links to the House Absolute; another hall, even wider, where standing shelves held disordered books links to the Library (I, chap. 6, 58); a narrow cell with a high, barred window and a straw-strewn floor links to the cell of Agilus (I, chap. 29, 251); a dark and narrow corridor lined with metal doors links to the Matachin Tower (I, chap. 29, 251).

18. The Examination

The portico of the Hall of Justice is crowded with people from Severian's past—they help him catch Zak. At the boulder, Severian chains himself rather than Zak. He waits for the trial to begin, surrounded by the crowd of sailors and those from his past, including the alzabo that ate Severa. Night falls. The crowd becomes agitated and begins fighting.

Echo: Series of pictures (125): scaffold at Saltus (II, chap. 4, 33); dark riverbank, probably the one with Dorcas and Jolenta (II, chap. 27, 254); roof of a tomb (II, chap. 30, 279); the Summer house, the final picture (III, chap. 12, 90).

Art Studies: Severian thinks the images (125-26) are "wrong" because each is from the non-Severian point of view (Cyriaca, Jolenta, Agia, etc.).

Echo: Hunna as half-boot victim (126) links to her scene (I, chap. 3, 29-30).

Paradox: Thecla inside and outside (127).

Animal Form: Zak sits like an atrox or some other great cat (128).

19. Silence

Unseen people free Severian and lead him behind the Seat of Justice to a narrow stair that exits the building. Apheta meets him and they walk through the quiet town of white marble. She convinces him that she is not human, rather she is a hierogrammate larva.

Language of Flowers: Moonvine (134) is a tropical white morning glory. Morning Glory means "Affectation."

Echo: Malrubius on beach (137) links to the Key of the Universe (IV, chap. 34, 278-80).

That's No Moon: "Something vast and bright—a moon, a Sun—was rising" (139) is the Ship seen from the world Yesod.

20. The Coiled Room

Severian follows Apheta into a room coiled like a nautilus shell. Apheta is glowing and they share a romantic interlude that results in the creation of the white fountain.

Myth: Apheta's self-generated light (141) is both a link to the Light Elves of mythology and the insect fireflies, which ties into term "larvae" (138). There is also a basic pattern mentioned by H. R. E. Davidson in *Myths and Symbols in Pagan Europe* (1988): "From time to time heroes in Irish or Welsh literature were drawn away to this realm out of time, lured by fair maidens in strange garb who enticed them into a mound or bore them away to an enchanted land across the sea" (113).

Echo: "[A]ppliances in Baldanders's castle" (141) links to that tower (III, chap. 23, 260).

Echo: A medley (143): Severian tells of sick girl in jacal, which links to that time in Thrax (III, chap. 8, 67); then about the Uhlan, a link to that episode on the green road (II, chap. 13, 108); then about Triskele, a link to his dog-doctoring time (I, chap. 4, 37); and finally about the dead steward episode, that links to an earlier chapter of this novel (V, chap. 6, 38).

Claw Notes: Apheta briefly tells Severian her guesses about the energy sources he drew upon in his healing attempts prior to leaving Urth (144). She describes three sources: himself, Urth, and Urth's old sun. She says he will be able to draw from the New Sun if he succeeds in the test. "When you were on the ship there was no world and no sun near enough, so you took what could be drawn from the ship itself, and nearly wrecked it. But even that was not sufficient [to resurrect the steward]" (144).

Art Studies: Apheta on the pictures, "You are a particularly monstrous monster" (146-47).

Mystery Solved: The one who tried to strike (131) was Purn (148).

21. Tzadkiel

The next day Severian goes to face the Hierogrammate Tzadkiel and finds Zak on the Seat of Justice, now metamorphosed into his hierogrammate form, like an angel with butterfly wings. Tzadkiel tells Severian that he has been tricked, there was no test. The Hierogrammates wanted to see the timeline Severian would forge, and having seen it, they know he is the New Sun. They will return Severian to Urth and the old planet will be destroyed at his command to make way for the new world.

The Urthman sailors in the audience draw their knives at this news—they attack and kill the Hierarch Venant identified as Tzadkiel's son. Again the aquastors (based upon people from Severian's past) fight against the sailors. Gunnie helps Severian, and the sailors are defeated. The aquastors dissolve.

Echo: A medley (150): memory leads to a tale about the angel Gabriel (I, chap. 18, 162); this triggers a second memory, that the tale was in the brown book, which alludes to when he first obtained that tome (I, chap. 6, 64); thoughts on powerful books triggers a memory of *The Book of Mirrors* in the House Absolute (II, chap. 21, 186). Another medley (151): a thought on how a species changes through time leads to memories of the time-altered man-apes in the Saltus Mine (II, chap. 6, 51); the preamble to a question for Tzadkiel leads to the memory of the angel in Melito's story (IV, chap. 9).

Echo: "[W]hich will be destroyed at your order" (153) links, in a distorted way, to a part in the play where the autarch tries to burn the "new seed": "May never the New Sun see what we do here [. . . .] ships! Sweep over us with flame till all is sere" (II, chap. 24, 227).

Echo: "[S]weat sprang . . . as blood had" (154) leads to the episode of *The Book of Mirrors* (II, chap. 21, 188). Malrubius and Triskele (155) link to the dissolve on the beach (IV, chap. 31, 251).

22. Descent

After answering questions, Apheta leads Severian and Gunnie beneath the surface of the world Yesod.

Proust: Apheta says, "Your race and ours are, perhaps, no more than each other's reproductive mechanisms" (159). This reminds me of a passage from *Cities of the Plain* (1922):

> Like so many creatures of the animal and vegetable kingdoms, like the plant which would produce vanilla but, because in its structure the male organ is separated by a partition from the female, remains sterile unless the hummingbirds or certain tiny bees convey the pollen from one to the other, or man fertilises them by artificial means. (*Cities of the Plain,* p. 650)

Art Studies: Apheta gives the official view of the pictures "Some recalled your duty. Others were meant to show you that you yourself had often meted out the harshest justice" (161).

23. The Ship

Gunnie is hurt when she hears about the carnal relations between Severian and Apheta. Severian learns that the world is also a ship, and that most of the work happens inside. Gunnie becomes frightened, recognizing a form of Hell in Yesod. The two of them are teleported back into Briah space (normal space) near the ship of Tzadkiel, where they are spotted by sailors and hauled aboard. Severian discovers he is no longer lame.

Dante: Gunnie pretends to read the lintel as saying, *"No hope for those who enter here"* (165), which alludes to *Inferno*, where the gate to Hell bears the famous inscription, "Abandon all hope, ye who enter here" (Canto III).

Jealousy: Gunnie's reaction to hearing about Severian and Apheta (166) provides a thematic link to Dorcas's reaction to Severian's tryst with Jolenta: "Dorcas wept in private, vanishing for a time only to emerge with inflamed eyes and a heroine's smile" (II, chap. 23, 209).

24. The Captain

A group of Hierodules, wearing their customary human masks, escorts the pair to meet the captain, the giantess Hierogrammate Tzadkiel. Severian is surprised that she does not recognize him, but then he realizes that they were thrust into the past when they were teleported. The others are dismissed. Severian alone remains to tell his story. Tzadkiel forms a human-sized version of herself to guide Severian to his stateroom using secret passages that turn out to be links to and from the mysterious grassy fields.

Animal Form: Voice of Captain Tzadkiel like the purr of a smilodon (173).

Animal: Smilodon "that slew our bulls as wolves kill sheep" (173).

Telling the Tale Thus Far: Severian tells earlier Tzadkiel (173).

Echo: A "Second House"-type of structure within the Ship (175) links to the Second House within the House Absolute (II, chap. 20, 183); picture tricks on the Ship (175) link to the picture trick Severian encountered in the House Absolute (II, chap. 20, 181).

Chess: "Yours is a race of pawns" (176).

25. Passion and the Passageway

While Severian sleeps, Thecla visits him in physical form. Later on he is walking through the ship and realizes that what he sees around him is being manufactured for him and his passage. He tries to outrun the process and succeeds, entering an alien landscape before losing consciousness.

Paradox of Thecla: Inside and outside (177).

Meditation on Women: Severian admits he has abandoned them too easily (179).

26. Gunnie and Burgundofara

Severian wakes up and sees two versions of Gunnie: the middle-aged one he remembers and a younger one who still uses her full name Burgundofara. In examining this paradox, Severian admits that his newly repaired face is that of Apu-Punchau, and he explains the mysterious wrestling between Hildegrin, Apu-Punchau, and himself at the stone town. Gunnie tells Severian to take Burgundofara with him to Urth. Severian sees Barbatus and Famlimus another last/first time. Severian and Burgundofara leave the ship of Tzadkiel and board a tender outside of the orbit of Dis (Pluto), bound for Urth.

Operative Theory: "If you haven't been Apu-Punchau yet, you can't die!" (185)

Echo: Memory (186) links to his day of exile from the Old Citadel (I, chap. 14, 130).

27. The Return to Urth

The tender is captained by a Hierodule and crewed by human sailors. Severian is aware of a connection between himself and the White Fountain, a white hole still many light-years away and moving at relativistic (sub-light) speed. The time dilation experienced onboard the tender is very strong and they arrive at Urth in less than one day.

Meditation on Women: Severian's actions toward them less about his will and more about their attitude toward him (190).

Echo: Feeling the distance of the white fountain (192) evokes the feeling he had standing before the windows of Master Ash (IV, chap. 17, 131).

Brown Book Tidbit: On region of mist between the living and dead (195).

28. The Village Beside the Stream

Severian and Burgundofara are let off at a village called Vici. Severian meets Herena, a girl with a withered arm, and he is able to heal her.

Sea or Space: Severian describes the tender as "a trim pinnace—just such a vessel as might have lain alongside some wharf in Nessus" (196).

Bible: Severian shapes Herena's arm (201), analogous to when Jesus healed a man with a withered hand (Matthew 12: 9-13; Mark 3: 1-6; Luke 6: 6-11).

29. Among the Villagers

Severian has become a powerful healer. The next day he goes with Burgundofara and Harena to Gurgustii, another village, where he heals Declan, a sick man on his deathbed.

Wise for a Youngster: Burgundofara says, "They'll kill us eventually, you know" (204).

Bible: When Severian heals the tumor of Declan (205), it is like Jesus healing the man with dropsy (Luke 14: 1-6). For his part, Declan says a seraph visited him and healed him (207), a seraph being one of the seraphim, the highest rank of the nine angelic orders.

Urth-Powered: Power to heal drawn from the Urth itself, followed by the sick feeling he had after executing Agilus (205), links to that execution (I, chap. 31, 267).

Commentary: Herena as the Little Sister character (208).

30. Ceryx

The day after that finds the trio in Os, where Ceryx the Necromancer challenges Severian to a duel. Severian refuses and arranges passage to Nessus on a ship. Ceryx sends a zombie to attack him.

Myth: Ceryx, an obscure Greek god, was a son of Hermes. Like his father, he was a messenger of the gods ("Ceryx" means "herald"). The necromancer of Os, through his power of re-animating the dead, seems less a "messenger" and more a "psychopomp," or guide of the dead, another aspect of Hermes.

Nessus Geography: When Hadelin says "this side of the khan" (214), we sense he means the Khan of Night, across the river from Citadel Hill (I, chap. 2, 27).

31. Zama

Rather than destroying the zombie, Severian heals it into a living man. He makes friends with the young man, whose name is Zama.

Echo: "[T]he poor volunteer [the axman] . . . had returned, and I was paralyzed with terror and guilt" (217) links back to the fight at the necropolis and the axman he had killed without later remorse (I, chap. 1, 16).

White Fountain Powered: Severian has power now (218), in contrast to when he was using Urth energy. His star is in the night sky at this time (220), not blocked by Urth's bulk.

32. To the Alcyone

Burgundofara spends the night with Hadelin the ship captain. In the morning they all go to the ship and Ceryx appears again. Zama attacks and kills Ceryx, then the townsmen kill Zama. Severian feels sickened.

Echo: Sight of locust flier leads to memory of pentadactyls (227), linking to that fearful encounter (IV, chap. 21, 166).

Multiple Severians in the Same Room: "Often I have dreamed of going back, and perhaps sometime I shall. Certainly more guests came to our aid when Zama broke our door. . . Indeed it sometimes seems to me that I caught a glimpse of my own face" (227).

An Ambiguous Result: Ceryx reanimated Zama to attack Severian. Severian responded by fully resurrecting Zama, and in doing this, it seemed he had won the contest; but then Zama killed Ceryx in berserk frenzy, and the crowd killed Zama. It is all a mess, but it seems Severian did not win the contest as cleanly as initially thought, and in fact he may have lost the contest with Ceryx, because Zama was still the berserk killer beneath a veneer of resurrection calm.

33. Aboard the Alcyone

On the ship, Severian tells himself the brown book tale "The Tale of the Town That Forgot Fauna."

Long ago, nine men went searching for a site to build a new city. They found a perfect place, inhabited only by an old woman. They offered her some money, but she refused. They offered her all their money, but again she refused. The leader warned her about the other men, and she gave the land to them on the condition that they build a garden in the middle, with a statue of her in the center. They agreed, but they made only a small garden with a wooden statue. The town grew in size but decayed in spirit. Eventually the garden was covered with warehouses, and the statue was burned as firewood. Then there was social upheaval, and the town burned down, yet it is said that an old woman remains, with a garden at the center.

Finishing the telling, Severian finds that Declan and Herena have come aboard to follow him against his orders. Declan says Severian pronounced a doom on Os.

Echo: Pulled up his hood (231), a link to his day of exile (I, chap. 14, 130).

Brown Book Tale: "The Town that Forgot Fauna" (232-35).

Vocabulary: A "godown" (234) is a warehouse, especially one in South or Southeast Asia or East Africa.

Bible: Severian's curse on the town of Os is perhaps similar to the curse Jesus laid upon the towns Chorazin and Bethsaida for ignoring the miracles he had performed there (Matthew 11:21; Luke 10:13). Declan and Herena admit they had gone to Os in advance (236) and had spoken of Severian and the miracles (236-37), similar to the work done promoting Jesus by the man formerly known as Legion, among others.

Commentary: This brown book tale resists the type of analytic tools that unlocked "The Tale of the Student and His Son" and "The Tale of the Boy Called Frog." There is a hint of Americana in the purchase of the land, being somewhat like the island of Manhattan bought by Dutch merchants from the natives (AD 1626); and the notion of a centrally located garden again evokes Manhattan, this time through its Central Park (AD 1858).

34. Saltus Again

The ship is caught in a sudden storm that threatens to capsize it. The first mate begs Severian to make it stop, even offering to kill the captain for sleeping with Burgundofara. Declan and Herena plead also. Severian comes to realize they are all correct: he had unconsciously called up the storm. He quiets it with a word, drawing back into himself the emotions he had denied.

The ship arrives in Saltus, but Severian cannot quite recognize the village. He has two new followers, and he asks one if there were no mines in the area. The sailor tells him one has just been started about a year before. Suddenly soldiers enter the inn and demand to be shown the Conciliator. Burgundofara points out Severian.

Regency Revealed: Severian wonders who is the suzerain who had replaced Father Inire (239), showing who was assigned to the job of regent during Severian's voyage to Yesod.

Jealousy: Severian had unconsciously called up the storm through his emotional state, including jealousy over Burgundofara and Hadelin.

Bible: Severian calms the storm (241-42), somewhat similar to when Jesus calmed the storm (Matthew 8:23-27; Mark 4:35-41; Luke 8:22-25).

Echo: Tramp of booted feet (245) recalls kelau at Saltus (II, chap. 1, 11).

Bible: When Burgundofara points him out to the soldiers (245), this parallels Judas betraying Jesus to the soldiers (Matthew 26:47-50; Mark 14: 43-45).

Commentary: Notice how the chapter title telegraphs to the reader information in advance of Severian's discovery. This is a different pattern.

35. Nessus Again

Severian kills three soldiers before they take him down. Another has a broken neck. Severian tries to heal himself using the White Fountain, but cannot, so he channels Urth's energies instead.

The soldiers take him by powerboat to Nessus. On the way he repairs the broken neck of the wounded soldier.

Echo: Soldiers with sympathy remind Severian (247) of that part in the play "Eschatology and Genesis" where guardsmen sought to protect Meschiane (II, chap. 23, 229).

Bible: When Severian falls a third time and is helped up by strangers (247), this half-echoes when Jesus faltered and was helped by Simon who carried his cross for a time (Matthew 27:32; Mark 15:21; Luke 23:26). Severian healing the soldier he had wounded (250) half-echoes when Jesus healed the ear of the soldier Peter had wounded (Luke 22:50-51), shortly after Judas identified Jesus to the same soldiers. The taking of Severian's clothing (251) links to the gospels telling of how soldiers took the clothing of Jesus (Matthew 27:35; Mark 15:24; Luke 23:34).

Dickens: "One of the hulks there has been fitted up to hold prisoners" (251) is a direct allusion to the prison hulks of *Great Expectations*.

36. The Citadel Again

At Nessus the soldiers take Severian to a prison, which he suddenly recognizes as the Citadel of the Autarch. But it is much newer in appearance, so he must be in the time long before his birth. He kills the sadistic leader of the jailers and tries to flee but is struck down by weaponry fired from the Matachin Tower. Miraculously he survives: the physician says that an earthquake hit at just the same moment, saving Severian's life by spoiling the gunner's aim.

Creating Guild Culture: Severian arrives wearing a dark cape (donated by his arresting officer (chap. 35, 251)) and no shirt at a time when the jailers have a strange uniform (256). The prohibition of women in the guild by Ymar (I, chap. 2, 20) is found to stem from this one bad apple among the jailers. Her sudden removal begins the process of reforming the sadistic jailers into impartial torturers (I, chap. 2, 19).

Echo: Memory of Cyriaca (257) links to the Summer house (III, chap. 12, 90); the quote from the play's Jahi, responding to the ground shaking, "The end of Urth, you fool" (259), links to that scene (II, chap. 24, 219).

37. The Book of the New Sun

Severian meets Reechy, an apprentice jailer who brings him his food and gives him some coins. The next morning Burgundofara and Captain Hadelin visit. Burgundofara begs forgiveness and Severian forgives her. In the evening his four followers visit and he tells them a long story so they will not despair when he is gone. Canog, a prisoner in the next cell, writes it down as *The Book of the New Sun,* which will become the holy text for the Church of the Conciliator, and the source of Talos's play.

Creating Guild Culture: Reechy throws coins before Severian after he has killed the leader of the jailers (261), links to "The chiliarch had tried to hand me my fee instead of casting it on the ground at my feet (as is customary)" (I, chap. 31, 266).

Animal Form: Burgundofara as red roe (263).

Tales of the Conciliator: Burgundofara to tell her future children about Severian (263). This could lead to inclusion in Canog's book.

Echo: Canog says, "[I]t should make a capital little book whenever I'm released" (266), a link to the fourth book requested by Thecla in her cell (I, chap. 6, 67). See also Wolfe's "Books in *The Book of the New Sun*" article, collected in Wright's *Shadows of the New Sun*.

38. To the Tomb of the Monarch

The next morning Severian learns that "Reechy" is just the boy's nickname: his real name is Ymar. Severian realizes that he is the one destined to become the first autarch. Severian is taken by flier to meet the monarch of the world at a mountain that is being carved into his likeness to serve as his tomb. The monarch is Typhon.

Bible: The brown book passage beginning *"Behold, I have dreamed a dream more"* (267), is from Genesis 37:9, dealing with Joseph who started with great expectations but spent time in prison before being taken to aid Pharaoh (Genesis 41).

Carved Mountains: Severian writes of the mountain carven likenesses of men and women (271), establishing that there are female autarchs.

Revenge: "Before the day was over, the knife thrust into the top of my boot would end a life" (271).

39. The Claw of the Conciliator Again

Severian is detained on an isolated part of the mountain. He frees and befriends a chiliarch who had treated him badly. When this chiliarch's troopers arrive they decide to desert the army with their commander. As a parting gift, Severian gives them the rose thorn he has kept since his encounter with Master Malrubius on the beach: in essence, he gives them the Claw of the Conciliator (the thorn coated with his blood). Then he steps off a cliff and into another world.

Animal Form: Typhon as yellow beard snake (274).

Revenge: "In that one afternoon I had as much vengeance as I wish ever to have" (276).

Echo: Memory (276) of freeing a bound smilodon (II, chap. 29, 270); recollection (280) of the Vodalus flier at the beginning of Severian's narrative (I, chap. 1, 17).

Kabbalah: Sephiroth (281) are the ten emanations of God, and one of them is named Yesod ("foundation").

Paradoxes to Perfect Memory: The return of the manskin sack (279).

40. The Brook Beyond Briah

Severian finds himself on the grass beside the Brook Madregot. He talks with a tiny version of Tzadkiel, who has been banished from the main body and will not tell Severian her name or why she was banished. He asks her how to get back to his proper time and place. She tells him and he goes.

Echo: Memory (283) of a stream in Orithyia and the pugmarks beside it (IV, chap. 1, 11).

Telling the Tale Thus Far: Severian tells his story to the exiled Tzadkiel (283).

Echo: Tell (284) of small angel and Gabriel in the brown book (I, chap. 18, 162); references again (287).

41. Severian from His Cenotaph

Severian winds up on the grounds of the House Absolute near a cenotaph erected in his memory. He enters the Second House and accidentally resurrects a long-dead assassin.

Edgar Rice Burroughs: In *A Princess of Mars* (1912), John Carter uses his tomb as a transit point between worlds like Severian (289).

Thematic Echo: This cenotaph is a thematic link to the opened door of the mausoleum (I, chap. 2, 21).

Animal: An antlered buck (289).

Operating Theory: The sequential order of mausoleum builder before stone town (290).

Echo: The cenotaph is located at the site where the play was performed (290), a link to that show (II, chap. 23, 209).

Echo Untraced: Severian seeing a woman from the loggia (293), though he does not explicitly make the connection, links to the scene from the play "Eschatology and Genesis" where the Contessa reports having seen a man from the loggia (II, chap. 24, 228). Note that in the play the Contessa sees the colonists in an earlier scene (II, chap. 24, 216).

42. Ding, Dong, Ding!

Severian goes into the throne room and sees a crisis unfolding.

Echo: The prophetess (296) is acting out a role from the play (II, chap. 24, 221-23); she also links to the girl in the jacal (297), since she was that girl (III, chap. 8, 67). The soldier's line, "Cacogens have landed a man and a woman" (301), links to the opening of the play (II, chap. 24, 211).

Timestamp: Baldanders says he has been living underwater for fifty years (300).

43. The Evening Tide

Revealing himself, Severian learns he has returned to Urth forty years after he had left on the trip to Yesod, arriving at the moment of the Commonwealth's destruction. The city Nessus had drowned two days before. In the chaos of these revelations, the resurrected assassin enters and kills Autarchia Valeria. Severian loses his healing powers.

Time Loop: Severian inadvertently (305-6) inspires the undine to save him back at the beginning of his adventure (I, chap. 2, 25).

Bible: Catch Catodon (306), where this is another name for Leviathan, an echo of "Canst thou draw out leviathan with an hook?" (Job 41:1).

The Odyssey: Odysseus's homecoming reversed. In Homer's work, the hero is not recognized upon sight by his wife; in Severian's case, the wife is the changed one. Odysseus sets out to "clean house" of rivals and traitorous maids; Severian arrives as the planet is washed, and Valeria is stabbed before him.

44. The Morning Tide

Urth is destroyed and reborn as Ushas, the world of the New Sun. Severian falls in with some survivors of the deluge (Odilo, Thais, and Pega) floating on a raft of debris.

Roles of the Autarch: Severian has a commission in the Black Tarantines (312). This curious detail links to the Tarantines of the Third Battle of Orithyia (IV, chap. 35, 288) as well as "The Tale of the Student and His Son" where mention is made of helots (II, chap. 17, 145).

Tarantine Cavalry: An ancient type, Tarantine cavalry units were famous for unique battle tactics, being the only cavalry of Hellenistic armies to use pure, advanced skirmishing tactics. Unarmored, first they would skirmish by hurling javelins at the enemy, followed with a charge. Tarantines were light cavalry; cataphracts were heavy cavalry. Proper Tarantines used javelins and avoided charges; the assumed Tartarines at Orithyia (IV, chap. 22, 172) are unarmored and have lancegays, but they charge.

Echo: Odilo gives a secondhand version of the first meeting between his father Odilo and the torturer Severian (313-14), echoing the event Severian had recounted (II, chap. 19, 171-74). Odilo says the torturer was scarred on the cheek (314), but that scarring came later (IV, chap. 26, 213).

Jealousy: When Pega mentions Valeria had remarried (315), this triggers in Severian the sort of dark feelings that prompted Odysseus to kill all the suitors and treacherous maids of his household. Yet for Severian it comes after the fact.

Semi-Validation of a Quasi-Vision: The situation of the survivors on the makeshift raft in this chapter is rather close to Severian's waking vision of being in a boat rowed through a drowned citadel (II, chap. 9, 76), yet also different enough. This follows the pattern of the vision of Severian riding the flying mount (I, chap. 15, 139-40) versus the reality of Severian being gripped by the flying mount (IV, chap. 25, 211).

45. The Boat

The four survivors are rescued by a boat piloted by an old sailor.

Echo: Allusion to balancing (317) references riding Vodalus's baluchiter on his fateful trip from village through mine trailings to forest (II, chap. 9, 76).

46. The Runaway

The old sailor turns out to be Eata, Severian's boyhood friend.

Echo: Hearing about Maxellindis's uncle dying at a bar table, Severian quotes a line, 'Men to whom wine had brought death long before lay by springs of wine and drank still, too stupified to know their lives were past' (326). This quote is a passage from "The Tale of the Student and His Son" in the brown book (II, chap. 17, 152), revealed by Marc Aramini in his article on "The Map" in *Between Light and Shadow* (2015).

Jealousy: Valeria's remarriage to Dux Caesidus (328).

Look-Alike: Eata's note that Dux Caesidus looked like Severian, "But he was handsomer . . . and maybe a little taller" (329), provides possibly spurious echoes from the crowd at the inn (V, chap 32, 227) and the empty coffins of the mausoleum (I, chap. 2, 21).

Telling the Tale Thus Far: Story time for Eata (329) ends at the Idas stabbing (V, chap. 7, 51).

47. The Sunken City

While the others sleep, Severian leaves the boat to swim in the water, no longer needing to breathe. He explores sunken Nessus.

William Hope Hodgson: Under the water, Severian sees immense monsters, "one was a living head without a body, another had a hundred heads" (332), which sounds like the landscape of Hodgson's *The Night Land* (1912).

Echo: "The locked and rusted gate . . ." (334) alludes to the second sentence of the first paragraph (I, chap. 1, 9); the ceremony in the previous frame tale foretold this moment (334), a link to the orbiting skulls (IV, chap. 28, 226). The Talarican quote (334) links to the conversation with the lochage at the bridge on the first night of his exile (I, chap. 14, 134).

The mausoleum door now closed "completed a motion begun . . . a century ago" (335) links to the door at first sight (I, chap. 2, 21). This means the door began closing fifty years before Severian's reign, which puts it around the time when Dorcas died. Let me expand upon this: the mausoleum has details covered in this guide, but one point not mentioned is the presence of two empty coffins. Given the context of the first chapter's grave robbing, one naturally assumes that the empty coffins of chapter 2 are signs of the same. In the larger context of Severian's narrative, it is also possible that the coffins were always empty, but there is the tantalizing potential that their corpses were resurrected. In summary, two persons left their coffins, exited Severian's mausoleum, and then Dorcas died. Perhaps they killed Dorcas, but it seems certain that they convinced her grieving husband to place her body in the Lake of Birds, since that is the important thing.

48. Old Lands and New

When Severian returns to the surface, Eata's boat is gone. He finds a more ancient sunken city that remains nameless. He meets Juturna again and she points out the way to the corridors of Time.

Echo: Memory (336) links to star gazing after fleeing Thrax (III, chap. 13, 100). Quotes of the play (339) link to lines from First Demon ("The continents themselves . . .") and Second Demon ("And from the sea . . .") talking to The Autarch (II, chap. 24, 226). "Lift, oh, lift me to the fallen wood" (339) links to both the ford (II, chap. 27, 255) and the lyrics written on the mirror in Thrax (III, chap. 4, 33-34), and thereby reveals that these are the same song, the one "about a girl who wanders through a grove in spring, lonely for her friends of the year before, the fallen leaves" (II, chap. 27, 255). Apheta looking down from the sky (340) like she had when he left Yesod (V, chap. 23, 167).

Medley of Flying Mount Vision (340) links back to bedtime with Baldanders (I, chap. 15, 139-40).

Time-Lapse Suggestion: That the Citadel is now "half-submerged" (341) where before it seemed completely underwater.

49. Apu-Punchau

Severian responds by jumping into the corridor and running as far into the past as he can. He ends up with a tribe of primitive people and tries to help them. They become suspicious and try to test him, but when the arrival of sunlight is delayed for him in the Miracle of Apu-Punchau, they accept him as divine king.

Echo: Memory (343) links to the first evening of his exile (I, chap. 14, 130). Incomplete nature of the play, regarding Old Sun character as being in the character list but never seen in the performed play (II, chap. 24, 211).

Memory (344) links to the shabby inn with fish on bread (I, chap. 15, 136).

Telling the Tale Thus Far: Through pantomime (349-50).

50. Darkness in the House of Day

Decades go by. Severian finds he cannot enter the corridors of Time anymore. As Apu-Punchau he teaches the tribe many things. When he finally tries to leave them, they panic and kill him.

He wakes up inside his tomb. The hierodules Ossipago, Barbatus, and Famulimus are there. So is the corpse of Apu-Punchau. Severian realizes that he himself is a self-generating eidolon, a ghost capable of gaining substance to become an aquastor and eventually a material being. As if that were not enough, he discovers that he had actually died in the fall with Sidero on the ship of Tzadkiel (back in chapter 9). He is only stranded in the era of Apu-Punchau until the first light from the White Fountain reaches Urth.

Meanwhile, the corpse begins to breathe.

Echo: "With light—the god from the machine" (353) a link to when Malrubius alluded to *deus ex machina* (IV, chap. 30, 243).

Telling the Tale Thus Far: To the hierodules (358).

Echo: The Ava quote (361) links to the Ava chapter (I, chap. 10, 81). The epigraph from Fitzgerald "Awake! for Morning in the Bowl of Night . . ." is quoted by Famulimus (361).

Eidolons: "Our eidolons are always of the dead" (361), so Triskele is dead.

51. The Urth of the New Sun

The danger to Severian is enormous, for a similar situation obliterated Hildegrin. Severian should not destroy the corpse, but he also does not want to be too close to it. Luckily enough, he escapes into the corridors of Time at the first possible moment and runs up to Ushas. There he finds an island of people who worship four gods named Odilo, Pega, Thais, and the Sleeper.

They recognize him as the Sleeper.

Echo: Memories (363) of the stone town encounter (II, chap. 31, 294).

Echo: A medley (364) of the first evening of his exile (I, chap. 14, 130); the tales told in the Pelerines' lazaretto (IV, chap. 7, chap. 9, chap. 11, chap. 13); the brief holiday with Valeria by the sea; his imprisonment in the jungle ziggurat (IV, chap. 26, 212); the year he spent among the Ascians; his flight from the white wolves in the House Absolute.

Apollo: Regarding Severian's year among the Ascians (364), Wolfe made a possibly related comment at the end of his interview by Robert Frazier about unwritten episodes of Severian: "And the year he spent as a slave of the Ascians" (Wright's *Shadows of the New Sun*, p. 55). Surprisingly there was a time when Apollo was sent by Zeus to be a slave in Troy for a year.

Language of Flowers: Lupine (voraciousness, imagination), loosestrife, white meadow rue (370).

Myth: "I had become the Oannes of these people!" (367) links to Oannes of the Lake People (III, chap. 31, 251).

Robert Graves: The sequel to *I, Claudius* (1934) is the lesser known *Claudius the God* (1935), which is highly relevant here.

Proust: *Time Regained* (1927) is the seventh, final, and posthumous volume of *Remembrance of Things Past*. With this section the tale accelerates through the Great War that destroys the aristocratic order of France and the society Proust had described. Despite this, the narrator discovers a method through memory and art to recapture a lost world.

Lawrence Durrell: Durrell's *Alexandria Quartet* (1957-60) is famous for offering "one dimension" (call them length, width, and depth) in each of the first three novels (*Justine, Balthazar,* and *Mountolive*), and in the final book (*Clea*) he shows change among these elements though time, the fourth dimension. *The Urth of the New Sun* provides a similar thing for *The Book of the New Sun*.

Appendix: The Miracle of Apu-Punchau

Gene Wolfe discusses the plausible explanations for Severian's prolonging of the night, and concludes the mostly likely is an eclipse of the Old Sun by the passage of some opaque body.

Echo: Link to note "That's No Moon" for chapter 19.

POSTLUDES FOR THE URTH OF THE NEW SUN

Urth Postlude 1: Eata's Life in Two Samples

Marc Aramini, in his work on the short story "The Map" in *Between Light and Shadow* (2015), has raised concerns that there are irreconcilable differences between Eata's life story as presented in "The Map" (*Endangered Species*, 20-36) and "The Runaway" (V, chap. 46). A large part has to do with what Aramini sees as discrepancies in the timelines described in the two works.

"The Map" is scant with time details:

- It is set during the Reign of Severian (*Endangered Species*, 20), which is taken to mean the ten years before he went to Yesod.
- Eata lost his lover Syntyche over the map (20).
- Syntyche was subsequently murdered over the map (28).
- Eata had lost his lover Maxellindis before (34).

"The Runaway" chapter of *The Urth of the New Sun* is far more detailed. It goes through the many phases of Eata's early years away from the guild, including:

- The estimated twenty weeks of courting Maxellindis before feast time, when Eata left the guild (325).
- The death of Maxellindis's uncle whereupon the pair inherited the boat (326).
- How, after a couple years, people thought they were married (326).
- How they were caught on a smuggling job, and Maxellindis went over the side (326), never to be seen again (327).
- The sending of Eata to Xanthic Lands (327).

- How his lover in Xanthic Lands was killed in a riot (so Syntyche was the third who had died, if we integrate the timelines).
- How when he come back to the Commonwealth, Eata bought a boat on shares, and has had it ever since (327).

Severian seeks to put years to it by saying, "If you stayed two years [in Xanthic Lands], you must have been eight with Maxellindis" (V, chap. 46, 328). (Obviously Severian is working to keep it within the ten-year frame.) To which Eata replies, "That would be about right. Four or five with her and her uncle, and two or three after, just us two on the boat" (328).

Presumably based upon Eata's rough calculation, Aramini writes about the seeming impossibility of placing "The Map" within the timeframe given in "The Runaway":

This [Maxellindis's death] occurred about eight years after the ascension of Severian, and then Eata was shipped . . . to the Xanthic Lands and did not return for over two years, at which point Severian was gone and Valeria was Autarchia.

But Aramini is using the greater numbers of Eata's rough estimate (5+3 = 8), and also stretching the time in Xanthic Lands to "over two years," implying (5+3+3 = 11). In contrast, by taking the lower numbers from Eata's sketch, he was with Maxellindis six years, gone the two years stated by Severian, returning in the last year or two before Severian left, and thus there is no conflict.

There are other details aside from the numbers of Eata's rough estimate. Aramini does not state it, but perhaps the "smoking gun" for his theory is a detail about the chrisos that Eata received when he returned to the Commonwealth: "So when I traded my extern gold for chrisos, some had your face on them and some hers, or anyway some woman's" (328). That certainly sounds convincing, as it implies that Valeria (or some woman) had assumed the throne already by the time Eata returned; but deeper reflection will recall that apprentice Severian thought his own first chrisos, the one given to him by Vodalus, had a woman's face on it (I, chap. 3, 31), yet it turned out to be the face of the old Autarch (chapter title "The Autarch's Face," chap. 3, 28). So it seems probable that the "woman's face" coins were the older coins in the group, rather than being newer coins.

Urth Postlude 2: The Big Twist

The surprise is that the coming of the New Sun triggers a deluge that washes the planet clean.

Instead of returning to the Commonwealth as a New-Sun king, Severian becomes a sort of accidental Utnapishtim, a survivor of the Babylonian Flood. It is fitting that he then becomes an Oannes to the new civilization, since Oannes is the one who warned Utnapishtim about the Babylonian Flood.

The events of the Urth Flood cast Doctor Talos's play "Eschatology and Genesis" in a new light. In *The Book of the New Sun,* the play seemed like an artist's mingling of the Bible's last book (Revelation, which deals with eschatology) and the Bible's first book (Genesis). Because Talos is said to have based his play on "certain parts of the lost *Book of the New Sun*" (II, chap. 24), the holy book of the Conciliator, one suspected that Talos was playing fast and loose with the material to provide entertaining novelty; yet the later events are remarkably close to the play, which in turn implies that the holy book he based it on really does end with eschatology followed by genesis.

So in this holy book, the figures of Meschia and Meschiane are signs of the apocalypse, rather like the star Wormwood in the book of Revelation, instead of being like Adam and Eve. Meschia and Meschiane are like Ash and Vine in Norse myth, coming after the end of the former world.

This reframing turns the tetralogy into the lead-up to the Noah Flood (Genesis 6:9-9:17), but one without a Noah or an ark. Urth is a wicked world washed clean of all evil, reseeded with Zoroastrian plant-man and plant-woman.

Thus "Eschatology and Genesis" can be seen more accurately as "The Eschatology *in* Genesis."

Urth Postlude 3: A Second Look at the First Severian

The Urth of the New Sun offers a big surprise when Severian becomes the Conciliator. This was unexpected, since while his future roles of mausoleum builder and Apu-Punchau had been well established in *The Book of the New Sun,* the Conciliator had remained distant and aloof, casting a sort of Aegis over Severian by way of the mysterious Claw which sometimes seemed to have a will of its own.

This third role for Severian opens a whole new can of paradoxes, beginning with a supposition that there was no Conciliator in the timeline of the first Severian. This finds strange support from the "he did not carry the Claw" bit by expanding it to "there was no Claw in existence."

There were only a few details about the first Severian in *The Book of the New Sun,* but they seemed solid. He was in Severian's future by at least ten years, because the hierodules Ossipago, Barbatus, and Famulimus came from his court in the future. He succeeded at bringing the New Sun, he built the mausoleum, and he died as Apu-Punchau.

This plan implied that Severian would intentionally perform actions having been done by the first Severian, in the same order: bring the New Sun, build the mausoleum, be Apu-Punchau.

Severian has no preparation for his role as the Conciliator. As a child he did not see a yearly play about the man, he has not performed in such a play, nor does it seem he has much studied him. So while we know something about Apu-Punchau and the mausoleum builder through their works, we know only about the Conciliator by how Severian, completely unprepared, performs the role.

His ministry on Urth lasts less than a week. One surprise is that he accidentally begins the reform of the old guild into the new guild, an act ascribed in the text to Ymar the Almost Just (I, chap. 2, 20). One implied action of the Conciliator is fulfilled when he gives away the Claw at the end of his ministry.

The text gives new clues as to what Severian expects to do next after finishing his writing in Ushas. *The Book of the New Sun* shows us Severian's life as torturer and autarch, with hints of his connections to Apu-Punchau, the Conciliator, and the anonymous dweller of the mausoleum. *The Urth of the New Sun* does a good job of making the first two connections lucidly clear, but it is silent on the mausoleum builder, presumably since it follows the pattern established by the other two. So it stands to reason that Severian leaves Ushas to have a career as an armiger during the reign of Ymar the Almost Just.

That he continues to travel in time is bolstered by the fact that Severian believes he saw his own face in the crowd of rescuers at the hotel in Os when he battled the zombie Zama (V, chap. 32, 227). In addition, there is his Ushas-written line directed to the reader, "[Y]ou, who were born upon Urth and have drawn your every breath there" (V, chap. 17, 118), which implies that Severian returned his manuscript to Urth and we are reading the Library's copy.

Speculative List

- Reign of Ymar: Build mausoleum (the symbols of fountain, ship, and rose suggest to me a trip to Yesod. That the flying ship symbol turns up on the old autarch's coin reinforces this, since he went to Yesod, and was the second after Ymar).
- Reign of Maxentius: Facilitate miracle of Katharine, then the mausoleum is sealed for thousands of years.
- Reign of Appian: Two mausoleum corpses are resurrected. One is the "bronze man," the model for the funeral bronze. They befriend Dorcas and her husband. When Dorcas dies, they convince her husband to place her in the Lake of Birds.
- Reign of Valeria: The exultant "bronze man" from the mausoleum travels the corridors of Time and becomes Dux Caesidius, to marry Valeria and keep her company for decades.
- Reign of Typhon: One or two Severians visit the hotel at Os to see the Conciliator pass through.

Urth Postlude 4: "Resurrect What You Kill" Redux

Returning to the theory that Severian can only resurrect those he has killed, to see how it is supported or diminished by the new information given in *The Urth of the New Sun*. This fringe theory acquires a new urgency after Severian has accidentally wiped out nearly all life on Urth.

The one resurrection anomaly of *The Book of the New Sun* has been resolved. Typhon's case was anomalous because it seemed there was no way Severian could be responsible for the Monarch's death so many chiliads in the past. The encounter with Typhon in *The Urth of the New Sun* resolves the anomaly by showing that Severian had caused Typhon's first death, which solidly places Typhon in the list of those killed and revived, making all six resurrections accounted for.

However, a new anomaly arises with Zama, the sailor reanimated by Ceryx and fully resurrected by Severian. When Severian turned the savage undead into the gentle resurrected, it seemed he had won the contest against Ceryx; but then Zama killed Ceryx in berserk frenzy, and the crowd killed Zama. The fact that the sailor had drowned on the river implies that Severian was not responsible for his first death, which seems as unassailable as the death of Typhon had been, yet soon after the second death of Zama we see Severian raising a storm that threatens to drown a ship, and we know there were other Severians at the hotel in Os. So the "anomaly" might resolve right there, with another Severian drowning Zama before the arrival of the Conciliator.

In *The Urth of the New Sun,* Severian continues to learn his power through trial and error. His failure to resurrect the murdered steward on Tzadkiel's starship (V, chap. 6) seems due to a lack of power, because Severian no longer has access to the white fountain (since the starship has passed out of Urth's universe). His effort leads to the disastrous blackout of the ship's energy grid. Later he achieves a breakthrough when he reshapes Harena's congenitally withered arm.

In the end Severian exists as a water god for the primitive people of Ushas, a sort of Apu-Punchau redux. He has the ability to time travel, but he has no other powers beyond that.

However, the "Resurrect What You Kill" theory offers the possibility that Severian embarks on a General Resurrection, raising everyone who died in the Deluge.

The first effect of this would be a "happy ending" to the series, in that the megadeath of the Deluge, while traumatic, was not permanent. This flows well with Severian's experience where, over the course of five books, he dies several times (some occasions more obvious than others), yet death is not an ending; resurrection is shown to be a kind of technology. But resurrection is traumatic, too, which adds qualifiers to the happy ending.

A General Resurrection is shocking, yet it follows from the rule of "raise only those you have killed" and the well-established fact that Severian killed countless numbers in the Deluge. One scrambles for objections: that Severian did not know those millions or billions of people (he did not know Triskele or Dorcas, so knowing the victim does not matter); that he lacks the energy (the New Sun, source of his energy, is now the primary star for Ushas); et cetera. If Severian were to resurrect someone on Ushas it seems logical that he would raise his fellow gods Pega, Thais, and Odillo, yet he does not seem to do so. Then again, as those three survived the Flood, Severian cannot raise them! (This could highlight the poignancy at the end of *The Urth of the New Sun* when Severian sees their graves.)

Additionally it means that there is more to Severian's education than simply feeling bad for causing the megadeath: he can do something to redress it. It also means that Urth's eschatology has the potential to be a great deal more like the Christian eschatology of Revelation than previously suspected.

However, there is evidence that Severian loses the healing powers at the Deluge, meaning that he cannot enact a General Resurrection. When he wakes up in the water after the assassin killed Valeria and himself, he takes stock and reports, "The inhuman power that [my body] had drawn from my star was gone . . . When I tried to reach the part of myself that had once been there, it was as though one who had lost a leg sought to move it" (V, chap. 44, 310). A few pages later, as storm clouds appear, he notes, "I . . . began to examine my emotional state before I remembered it could no longer be the power of my star that had summoned the clouds gathering in the east" (313).

Still, it seems that Severian was banking on such a thing, that a General Resurrection was an Ace hidden up his sleeve, to be used should all else fail in his poker game with the gods.

BIBLIOGRAPHY

SOURCE TEXT

Wolfe, Gene. *The Shadow of the Torturer.* New York: Simon and Shuster, 1980.

———. *The Claw of the Conciliator.* New York: Simon and Shuster, 1981.

———. *The Sword of the Lictor.* New York: Simon and Shuster, 1981.

———. *The Citadel of the Autarch.* New York: Simon and Shuster, 1983.

———. *The Urth of the New Sun.* New York: Tor, 1987.

———. *Endangered Species.* New York: Tor, 1989.

———. *Starwater Strains.* New York: Tor, 2005.

GENE WOLFE REFERENCE

Andre-Driussi, Michael. *Lexicon Urthus.* Second Edition. Albany, California: Sirius Fiction, 2008. [I, ch. 7, ch. 14; IV, ch. 7]

———. *Gene Wolfe: 14 Articles on His Fiction.* Albany, California: Sirius Fiction, 2016. [I, ch. 22, ch. 23, ch. 24; II, ch. 11]

Aramini, Marc. *Between Light and Shadow: An Exploration of the Fiction of Gene Wolfe, 1951 to 1986.* E-book edition. Kouvola, Finland: Castalia House, 2015. [V, ch. 46; Urth Postlude 1]

Clute, John. *Strokes.* Paperback edition. Seattle, Washington: Serconia Press, 1988. [I, ch. 2, ch. 4]

Feeley, Greg. "The Evidence of Things Not Shown: Family Romance in The Book of the New Sun." *New York Review of Science Fiction No. 31* and *32,* March and April, 1991. [I, ch. 1, ch. 4, ch. 23, ch. 35; III, ch. 20, ch. 26]

Gordon, Joan. *Gene Wolfe: Starmont Reader's Guide 29.* Mercer Island, Washington: Starmont House, 1986. [II, ch. 11]

Manlove, C. N. *Science Fiction: Ten Explorations*. Basingstoke, Hampshire: Macmillan, 1986. [I, ch. 1, ch. 5]

Wolfe, Gene. *Castle of Days*. New York: Tor, 1992. [I, epigraph, ch. 2, ch. 7, ch. 10, ch. 11, ch. 16, ch. 17; II, epigraph, ch. 18; III, epigraph, ch. 33; IV, epigraph]

Wright, Peter. *Attending Daedalus: Gene Wolfe, Artifice and the Reader*. Liverpool: University of Liverpool Press, 2003. [II, ch. 11]

Wright, Peter (ed.). *Shadows of the New Sun*. Paperback edition. Liverpool: University of Liverpool Press, 2007. Contains the following:

- Edwards, Malcolm. 1973 interview. [III, ch. 13]
- Frazier, Robert. 1983 interview. [I, ch. 17; V, ch. 51]
- Gordon, Joan. 1981 interview. [I, ch. 8, ch. 18]
- Jordan, James B. 1992 interview. [I, ch. 8]
- McCaffrey, Larry. 1988 interview. [I, ch. 8]
- Swanson, Elliott. 1986 *Interzone* interview. [II, ch. 16; IV, ch. 2; V, epigraph]
- Wolfe, Gene. "Books in *The Book of the New Sun*." [I, ch. 6; V, ch. 37]

REFERENCE

Davidson, H.R. Ellis. *Myths and Symbols in Pagan Europe*. Syracuse, New York: Syracuse University Press, 1988. [V, ch. 20]

Edwards, Malcolm and Robert Holdstock. *Realms of Fantasy*. Paperback edition. Olympic Marketing Corp, 1983. [I, ch. 1; II, ch. 21]

Greenaway, Kate. *Language of Flowers*. 1884. [I, ch. 6, ch. 10, ch. 19, ch. 20, ch. 24, ch. 25, ch. 30, ch. 32; II, ch. 8, ch. 14, ch. 21, ch. 22; III, ch.1, ch. 2; IV, ch. 19, ch. 31, ch. 32; *Empires of Foliage and Flower;* V, ch. 19, ch. 51]

Köster, Thomas. *50 Artists You Should Know*. New York: Prestel, 2006. [II, ch. 23]

Oxford Dictionary of Saints. Third Edition, paperback. 1992.

SECONDARY TEXTS

Aesop. "The Fighting Cocks and the Eagle." Circa 600 BC. [IV, ch. 9]

Arabian Nights. [III, ch. 6, ch. 13, ch. 17, "The God and His Man"]

Asimov, Isaac. "Runaround." 1942. [V, ch. 13]

Baum, L. Frank. *The Wonderful Wizard of Oz*. 1900. [II, ch. 15, ch. 18]

Bible. King James Version. [I, ch. 6, ch. 9, ch. 17, ch. 21, ch. 25, ch. 34; II, ch. 1, ch. 2, ch. 3, ch. 5, ch. 8, ch. 9, ch. 10, ch. 11, ch. 15, ch. 21, ch. 24, ch. 26, ch. 31; III, ch. 6, ch. 8, ch. 11, ch. 12, ch. 24, ch. 26, ch. 27, ch. 28, ch. 29, ch. 38; IV, ch. 9, ch. 11, ch. 13, ch. 14, ch. 19, ch. 31; "The God and His Man"; *Empires of Foliage and Flower;* V, ch. 12, ch. 15, ch. 28, ch. 29, ch. 33, ch. 34, ch. 35, ch. 38, ch. 43]

Blish, James. *Black Easter.* 1968. [III, ch. 26]

Borges, Jorge Luis. *The Book of Imaginary Beings.* 1957. [I, ch. 2, ch. 6, ch. 15, ch. 20; II, ch. 10; III, ch. 37]

"The Circular Ruins." 1940. [II, ch. 17]

———. "Doctor Brodie's Report." 1970. [I, ch. 2]

———. "Funes the Memorius." 1942. [I, ch. 2]

———. "The Library of Babel." 1941. [I, ch. 2]

———. "Rosendo's Tale." 1969. [I, ch. 2]

———. "Tlön, Uqbar, Orbis Tertius." 1941. [I, ch. 2]

Boswell. *Life of Samuel Johnson.* 1791. [I, ch. 6]

Budrys, Algis. *Rogue Moon.* 1960. [II, ch. 18]

———. *Who?* 1958. [II, ch. 18]

Bunyan, John. *The Pilgrim's Progress.* 1678. [I, ch. 17; II, ch. 3, ch. 14, ch. 18]

Burroughs, Edgar Rice. *A Princess of Mars.* 1912. [V, ch. 41]

Carroll, Lewis. *Through the Looking Glass.* 1871. [II, ch. 16; IV, ch. 22]

Chambers, Robert W. *The King in Yellow.* 1895. [I, ch. 21]

———. *The Maker of Moons.* 1896. [I, ch. 21]

Crane, Stephan. *The Red Badge of Courage.* 1895. [II, ch. 16; IV, ch. 1, ch. 22]

Crichton, Michael. *Eaters of the Dead.* Paperback edition. New York: Bantam Books, 1977. [II, ch. 6]

Dante, Alighieri. *Inferno.* 1320. [I, ch. 22, ch. 23; V, ch. 23]

———. *Paradiso.* [III, ch. 27]

Dickens, Charles. *Bleak House.* 1853. [I, ch. 16]

———. "A Christmas Carol." 1843. [III, ch. 32]

———. *Great Expectations.* 1861. [I, ch. 1, ch. 3, ch. 4; IV, ch. 38]

———. *The Pickwick Papers.* 1837. [I, ch. 35]

Doyle, Arthur Conan. *A Study in Scarlet.* 1887. [IV, ch. 33]

Durrell, Lawrence. *The Alexandria Quartet.* 1957-60. [V, ch. 51]

Eliot, T.S. "The Waste Land." 1922. [III, ch. 11]

Ellison, Harlan. "'Repent, Harlequin!' Said the Ticktockman." 1965. [III, ch. 20]

Fitzgerald, Edward. *The Rubaiyat of Omar Khayyam.* 1859. [V, epigraph, ch. 50]

Flaubert, G. *Salammbo.* 1862. [III, ch. 10]

Gibbon, Edward. *The History of the Decline and Fall of the Roman Empire.* 1776-89. [II, ch. 4]

Graves, Robert. *I, Claudius.* 1934. [I, ch. 1, ch. 23, ch. 28; IV, ch. 33; V, ch. 1]

———. *Claudius the God.* 1935. [V, ch. 51]

Heinlein, Robert A. "Universe." 1941. [V, ch. 10, ch. 11, ch. 14]

Hodgson, William Hope. *The Night Land.* 1912. [V, ch. 47]

Homer. *The Odyssey.* 8th century BC. [III, ch. 30; IV, ch. 43]

Horace. *The Satires.* 35 BC. [*Empires of Foliage and Flower*]

Japanese poem: "If a bird won't sing..." [IV, ch. 13]

Joyce, James. *Ulysses.* 1922. [I, ch. 16; II, ch. 24; III, ch. 30]

Kafka, Franz. "In the Penal Colony." 1919. [I, ch. 13]

Kipling, Rudyard. "The Dawn Wind." 1911. [IV, epigraph]

———. *The Jungle Book*. 1894. [III, ch. 19; The God and His Man]

———. *Stalky & Co*. 1899. [I, ch. 2]]

L'Engle, Madeleine. *A Wrinkle in Time*. 1962. [III, ch. 34]

Lindsay, David. *A Voyage to Arcturus*. 1920. [III, ch. 13-24]

"Little Red Riding Hood." [I, ch. 18; II, ch. 31; III, ch. 16; IV, ch. 19]

Marlowe, Christopher. "Doctor Faustus." 1592. [III, ch. 28; IV, ch. 33]

———. "Tamburlaine the Great." 1587. [V, ch. 1]

Mayhew, Henry. *London Labor and the London Poor*. 1851. [I, ch. 14, ch. 16]

Melville, Herman. *Moby Dick*. 1851. [I, ch. 1, ch. 15]

Milton, John. *Paradise Lost*. 1667. [I, ch. 1; IV, ch. 1]

Moorcock, Michael. "The Dreaming City." 1961. [IV, ch. 1]

Orwell, George. *Nineteen Eighty-Four*. 1949. [II, ch. 23]

Ovid. *Metamorphoses*. AD 8. [III, ch. 13; IV, ch. 35]

Petronius. *The Satyricon*. Late 1st century AD. [IV, ch. 35]

Pinocchio. [I, ch. 15, ch. 30]

Plato. *Apology*. [I, ch. 6]

———. *The Republic*. 380 BC. [III, ch. 38]

Peake, Mervyn. *Titus Groan*. 1945. [I, ch. 5, ch. 25]

Poe, Edgar Alan. "Annabel Lee." 1849. [I, ch. 2]

———. "MS. Found in a Bottle." 1833. [V, ch. 1]

———. "Tamerlane." 1827. [V, ch. 1]

Proust, Marcel. *Remembrance of Things Past: Vol. 1—Swann's Way & Within a Budding Grove*. Paperback. New York: Vintage, 1981. [I, ch. 9, ch. 24; II, ch. 10, ch. 13; Book Postlude 4]

———. *Remembrance of Things Past: Vol. 2—The Guermantes Way & Cities of the Plain*. Paperback. New York: Vintage, 1981. [V, ch. 22]

———. *Remembrance of Things Past: Vol. 3—The Captive, The Fugitive & Time Regained*. Paperback. New York: Vintage, 1981. [I, ch. 8; III, ch. 25] [II, ch. 7] [V, ch. 51]

Pynchon, Thomas. *The Crying of Lot 49*. 1966 [II, ch. 24]

Sandars, N. K. *The Epic of Gilgamesh*. Paperback. Harmondsworth, England: Penguin Books, 1983.

Shakespeare. "Romeo and Juliet." 1595. [I, ch. 6]

———. "Twelfth Night." 1602. [I, ch. 4]

Shelly, Mary. *Frankenstein*. 1818. [III, ch. 35]

Smith, Clark Ashton. *Xothique*. Paperback edition. New York: Ballantine Books, 1970. [I, ch. 2; II, ch. 31]

Sophocles. *Antigone*. 441 BC. [II, ch. 2]

Stout, Rex. *Fer-de-Lance*. 1934. [I, ch. 21, ch. 28]

Twain, Mark. *The Adventures of Tom Sawyer*. 1876. [I, ch. 1]

Van Gulik, Robert. *Celebrated Cases of Judge Dee*. Paperback. New York: Dover

Publications, 1976. [I, ch. 18]

Vance, Jack. *The Dying Earth.* 1950. [I, ch. 29, ch. 33; II, ch. 17, ch. 31; III, ch. 5, ch. 16, ch. 33; IV, ch. 27; The God and His Man]

——. *The Eyes of the Overworld.* 1966. [I, ch. 30; III, ch. 11, ch. 26, ch. 28]

——. "The Seventeen Virgins." 1974. [I, ch. 30]

von Le Fort, Gertrud. "Return to the Church." 1924. [II, epigraph]

Walpole, Horace. *The Castle of Otranto.* 1764. [I, Appendix]

Watts, Isaac. "Psalm XC." 1719. [I, epigraph]

Wells, H. G. *The Island of Doctor Moreau.* 1896. [II, ch. 8]

——. *The Time Machine.* 1895. [III, ch. 35]

ABOUT THE AUTHOR

Michael Andre-Driussi has produced a number of books about science fiction and fantasy works. His titles on Gene Wolfe's fiction are *Lexicon Urthus* (1994), *The Wizard Knight Companion* (2009), *Gate of Horn, Book of Silk* (2012), and *Gene Wolfe: 14 Articles on His Fiction* (2016). With Alice K. Turner he co-edited *Snake's-Hands: The Fiction of John Crowley* (2001). His two books about Jack Vance's oeuvre are *Handbook of Vance Space* (2014) and *Jack Vance: Seven Articles on His Work and Travels* (2016). Branching out, he also has touched on Soviet science fiction with the popular *Roadside Picnic Revisited* (2016), being about the Strugatsky novel made into the Russian motion picture *Stalker* (1979), as well as a survey of Japanese animation in *True SF Anime* (2014).

Made in the USA
Monee, IL
16 January 2020